MASTODON

STEVE STRED

Mastodon

Steve Stred

Cover art by François Vaillancourt

Edited by David Sodergren

Formatted by David Sodergren

1st Edition

Black Void Publishing

Ebook ISBN: 978-1-990260-06-3

Paperback ISBN: 978-1-990260-42-1

Hardcover ISBN: 978-1-990260-08-7

ADVANCE PRAISE FOR MASTODON

"An old-school creature thriller told with crisp pacing and kick-ass set pieces, Steve Stred's Mastodon is a monster-in-the-woods tale with some choice surprises and plenty of rampaging fun."

Andrew Pyper, author of *The Residence*, *The Damned* and *The Demonologist*

"Steve Stred's Mastodon reads like a cross between Gary Paulson's Hatchet and Jeff Vandermeer's Southern Reach Trilogy: a big-hearted adventure yarn with a dark and compelling mystery at its core."

Shaun Hamill, author of *A Cosmology of Monsters*

"Mysterious. Gripping. High-octane. Mastodon is not the typical creature feature."

Eddie Generous, author of *Rawr* and *Behemoth Risen*

"Mastodon is a jaw-dropping trek into a heart of darkness. Full of emotion, yet rife with grotesque imagery that only Stred can deliver."

David Sodergren, author of *The Forgotten Island* and *Maggie's Grave*

"Mastodon is another tour de force from Canada's master of dread. The journey into a forbidden wilderness cordoned off by the military is reminiscent of Jeff Vandermeer's Annihilation, but as bleak, daring, and darkly comic as Harlan Ellison. The pace of the story never relents, its emotional highs are spectacular, and its lows will rip your guts out: a voyage and return epic with the balls-to-the-wall horror shows of S. C. Mendes's The City thrown in. Stred should be held in the same regard as Straub and King."

Joseph Sale, author of *Save Game* and *Gods of the Black Gate*

"Mastodon is a compelling read that will leave you blistered and broken as you join a young man's rescue mission into the Canadian wilderness inhabited by unspeakable horrors. Steve Stred masterfully delivers a story exploring the physical and emotional limits we push through in order to save the people we hold most dear."

J. A. Sullivan, horror writer and contributor to Kendall Reviews.

For OJ.
We miss you so much buddy.
I hope you knew just how much you were loved.
You were the best dog.

1

JUNE 1ST, 1990

THE HOWLING OF WIND ACCOMPANIED BY THE SOUND OF RAIN brought her back.

She came to in a cave, naked.

Pain rolled across her body as she moved.

This was followed by the throbbing pulse in her head. Reaching to the back of her skull, she felt a goose-egg poking through her matted hair, the area sore to the touch. Her hands shook, her skin wrinkled and cold from exposure. She was shivering, the wind whipping into the dark space where she sat.

She ached all over, unsure what had happened, where she was, or even *who* she was. Her knees were in rough shape. She wanted to touch the area but was afraid of what she'd find. She was bleeding heavily, and knew she needed medical attention. Her current location suggested that wasn't going to happen.

The pattering of rain hitting rocks grabbed her attention. Looking towards the light source of the cave, she saw the opening of her rocky cage.

She shuffled forward, unable to fully stand. Her bare

feet didn't appreciate the bite of the surface, but she ignored it, wanting to see just what type of imprisonment she'd been tossed in.

The entrance to the cave was blocked by thick branches, lashed together by thicker, rough rope. She grasped the bars, pushing and pulling but finding no give. Beyond, the rain continued, accompanied by another gust of wind, the trees that surrounded the cave using their roots to hold firm against Mother Nature's onslaught.

Feeling her eyes well up, she returned to the back wall, shocked by the sudden realization that her breasts were leaking.

Looking at her nipples, she found cream colored fluid dripping out in a steady stream. She cupped the tissue around, applying pressure towards her areola, and watched as more of the fluid trickled out of her nipples.

Why was she lactating?

She tenderly explored her stomach, desperately trying to let her fingertips bring forth some sort of memory, something to tell her what had happened. Her loose skin and belly button told her that something had been in her recently. Her fingers travelled lower, further south, across her dark patch of hair. Once there, she probed softly. Each contact of finger to fold created pain. When she brought her hand up, she saw the tips covered in red.

The child that had been within had been birthed recently.

"Where's my baby?"

She said it aloud, spoke it to the wind and the woods.

Finding no reply, she yelled it, she screamed it, until snot caked her lips and the tears became so cold she couldn't open her eyes.

She pulled herself back against the closest thing to a

corner in the cave, wrapping her arms around her legs as she forced them painfully against her engorged chest.

Still, the only noise she heard was the rain hitting rock and the wind whistling through the trees.

As she huddled to generate some warmth, two names whispered over-and-over in her head. Putting one finger to the wall, she began to use her nail to carve them.

2

GOLDEN STAR JUNE 3RD, 1990

RCMP STRUGGLE FOR CLUES FROM MISSING MOTHER.

RCMP are seeking input from the community regarding the strange disappearance of Sandra Barton. Sandra and her husband Neil, along with their three-month-old son, Tyler, were hiking near Ogre Peak and Amiskwi Peak, approximately 300 kms (185 miles) North East of Golden.

Two days ago, Neil, carrying Tyler, flagged down a forestry helicopter, where Neil related that during the night, Sandra had stepped away for a moment. When noises and her screams alerted Neil to something happening, he rushed in the direction she'd gone, but came up empty handed. The next day, he searched but found nothing of note. Police have confirmed that when they arrived at the campsite, no blood was found and that Neil's story checked out. He is not considered a person of interest.

Because of Sandra's extensive backcountry skills, RCMP believe that she may still be alive and are asking for volunteer hikers to join them on an overnight hike into the area to search for her.

. . .

Golden Star, June 10th, 1990

RCMP and Canadian Forces call off search for Sandra Barton.

With no leads or signs discovered, RCMP — with the assistance of Canadian Forces — have called off the search for missing hiker and new mother, Sandra Barton.

Multiple overnight searches have taken place, but with nothing giving the searchers any clues as to her whereabouts, the decision was made.

"It's something we don't take lightly," Constable Ron Carson said, "but the reality is, we just don't have the finances or the manpower to continue doing full scale searches. A week in the wild is survivable, especially by someone with Sandra's skills. We'll keep our eyes open for any signs and have been in touch with local Conservation Officers so that they will contact us at the first indication of Sandra's whereabouts. If you are out hiking and notice anything, anything at all, please don't hesitate to contact us. Sometimes the smallest clue is all that is needed to break a case wide open."

Golden Star has reached out to Neil Barton but at the time of publication, no comment has been issued.

3

JUNE 1ST, 2007

17 YEARS LATER.

"THREE WEEKS OFF, EH NEIL? GOT ANY PLANS?"

Neil Barton looked over at his coworker Dave Sanders, giving the man a warm smile. Dave was a good guy, a hard-worker who loved watching football. A pleasure each and every day.

"Yeah, actually. Tyler and I are going to head out to Cultus Lake. I have a cabin lined up, and an old friend has a shop out there. Will be good to reconnect with him, but also we'll reconnect with the woods."

"Ha," Dave replied. "You guys spend more time in the woods than in your house. Reconnect to the woods, my ass." They both laughed, Dave giving Neil's shoulder a friendly punch.

"Got me there," Neil replied, shifting his gear bag under his feet.

"How much longer you going to do this?"

Neil looked back over at Dave, raising his eyebrows.

"Something I should know, Dave?"

"Nah, it's just, your boy's getting older. Thought you'd get sick of the fly-in-fly-out life."

"Hmmph. Not with the way they pay."

The small talk continued until it was time to board. The plane was always small, the passenger list even smaller. This flight consisted of only the pilot, Dave and Neil.

"Alright, gentlemen. Turbulence ahead, we have some downstream pressure coming at us. Flight time will be around three hours, hopefully less. You could try to sleep, but I doubt you'll get any."

Then the ground crewman, the only other person at the private airport, got the props spinning and within a matter of minutes the plane had sped down the runway and left the ground below.

Tyler finished up his last bit of studying for the day. To say he was excited that Grade 12 was coming to an end was an understatement. He'd already finished up three of his four finals, and with one more in two days, he'd be done. Completely finished High School. It should've felt momentous, something he'd remember forever as he entered into adulthood. Instead all he thought about was once the final exam was finished, they'd leave and by that afternoon they would be out at Cultus, on the deck of the cabin. His dad would be BBQing, they'd be in shorts, and neither would have a care in the world.

Leaning back in his chair, he thought about some of the camping trips and hikes they'd done over the years. So many great memories, but he knew that there were two reasons his dad had instilled such a love for the forests in him. The first were the life skills it gave him. The ability to start fires, live off the land, and not depend on power, water taps and grocery stores. The second, though, was the closer of the two to Neil Barton's heart. It was a way for his son to keep a connection with Sandra.

Tyler had looked at the photos of her and his dad a million times over the years. He'd smiled and touched them, trying to memorize every curve and ridge of her face, but photos never were that accurate, especially in the Polaroid days. He loved the photos of his mom, pregnant and hiking, still getting out into the woods. He knew some of the details of her disappearance, that they'd been camping when he was born, that his dad had told the authorities he was three months old on the night she'd disappeared, not a newborn. They never questioned it, too focused on the missing woman, but his dad had rushed Tyler to his aunt's place before returning to continue searching for his wife.

They never celebrated the anniversary of her disappearance, even though he knew it was today. June 1st hung around their heads like a noose at times, bringing forth smiles and tears all the same. Instead they celebrated her birthday. They'd have a little cake and look through the old photo albums until they were both too tired to look anymore.

Now, as he waited for his dad to let him know he'd touched down, he thought back to that night his mom disappeared, thinking about the details his dad had shared, and wished like anything that she was here today.

"This a normal amount of turbulence?"

Neil looked at Dave, glad his friend had asked the question, as the plane was bumping and lolling more than usual. They'd flown on these small planes hundreds of times over the years, in every weather imaginable, but this was different.

"No, it's not," the pilot replied. Neil could see the man sweating, his skinny arms fighting to control the craft.

BANG

A massive noise off to one side snapped Neil and Dave's heads over, both looking in horror as they realized just how low they were. The tops of the trees were now beside them, and as they turned back to the front, they watched as the forest began to engulf the plane as they crashed into the mountain side.

The pilot was impaled before Dave could even yell, a branch crashing through the windshield and spearing the man through his chest. The branch went clear through the front seat, missing Neil's arm by less than an inch.

The impact of the plane striking the trees spun the vessel sideways. It ricocheted like a pinball in an arcade game. The plane struck a thicker tree, which caused it to rotate and go end-over-end, Dave and Neil caught in a surreal weightless position as the plane seemingly rotated around their bodies.

They were both in midair, off their seats, when the plane struck the forest floor, the back section breaking off and the front section bursting into flames. Dave was ejected on impact, sent flying through the air away from the craft, his scream fading as he travelled further away. Neil was slammed into the front seat then thrown to the floor. Though he should have lost consciousness, the smell of flames and fuel kept him going, fighting the haze that threatened to pull him under.

Other than the crackle of the burning plane, all was quiet. The forest was eerily silent, the birds and animals having departed from the plane's intrusion.

"Ahhhhhhhhhhhh!"

A yell of pain broke the calm.

"Ahhhhhhhhhhh!"

The second scream sent a throb of blood to his ears, his heart racing even more as fear rushed through his body. Neil looked around, finding himself alone. He knew it was Dave. The pilot was slumped over the branch that had impaled him, his legs now beginning to burn. As inhumane as it was, Neil left him, knowing there was nothing he could do to bring the man back to life and as much as it would restore some dignity to the dead, he needed to attend to Dave and try and save the man.

Even though the back of the plane had snapped off, Neil was still trapped in the cabin of the plane, no opening accessible to climb out. He grabbed the small emergency exit window and forced it open, then slid through the gap, landing with a pained thud on the ground below.

He moved away from the plane as fast as he could, feeling the heat increasing as the flames travelled across the remains of the plane and grew higher. He hoped the burning craft would be enough to get the attention of hikers in the area or even forestry workers out doing summer snow level counts.

"Ahhhhhhhhhhh!"

The yell came again, and Neil started in the direction he thought it was coming from. He hadn't taken any time to inspect himself for injuries, but he figured if he was up and moving this well, whatever damage he'd suffered could wait.

Running through the trees, he caught movement beside him deeper in the woods, travelling at a high rate of speed. Neil had spent most of his forty-five years in the woods. Over that time, he'd developed an encyclopedic mind about everything in the forest; plants, nuts, mushrooms, trees, and animals. What was moving didn't register. The only thing that kept sneaking back into Neil's mind was *wolf,* but the size of the shape didn't add up.

Neil returned his focus to finding Dave. If his friend was screaming that loudly and in that much pain, he wouldn't have long until shock took over and if that happened, there'd be no saving the man, no matter how minor or major the injuries. This was the absolute worst location that someone could suffer an injury.

He exited the trees and arrived at the edge of a frozen river, the elevation high enough that snow bordered the water.

There along the shore, amongst the debris, was Dave. He was bent at a hideous angle, Neil noting that surely his spine would be pulverized, but the screaming was coming not from the injury, or the appearance of a long tree root protruding through his right shoulder. No, the screaming was coming from the pack of wolves that were rushing in to bite chunks off the man.

Neil stood in stunned silence when he realized that the wolves were not normal. Sure, grey and black wolves could grow to immense sizes, the grey growing to insane proportions of three feet high at the shoulder and six feet long. But the half dozen beasts that were making quick work of Dave's flesh were easily twice that size.

"Neil?"

A familiar woman's voice shot through him, taking him back all those years to the forest, to a life he'd long since believed was over. He turned and nearly dropped in shock when he saw Sandra standing at the edge of the woods, her face as pristine and beautiful as the day she'd disappeared.

"Sandra? How..."

Shaking the shock away from his eyes, he saw that it

wasn't completely her. Something was off. It was *her* voice and *her* face and *her* presence, but the rest of her he wasn't able to process.

"You shouldn't be here," she said.

From behind him came the crunch of footsteps and then all went black before he could even turn.

4

____

THE FOREST FLOOR BUMPED AND BANGED AGAINST NEIL'S BODY as he was dragged through the trees.

His head ached and pounded, the rough treatment not making it any better.

He could smell rotting meat and an odor that reminded him of a pig sty.

Looking at what was dragging him, he saw an immense figure, dark and hairy.

Neil tried to stand, to halt the progress, but his straining only revealed that his wrists were bound, his arms in front of him. He heard something behind him and craned his neck to see a man in dark fatigues keeping pace. He carried a large firearm, military issue of some sort, but Neil had trouble placing it. The man's face was hidden by a mask, but when he noticed Neil looking at him, he took a quick step and brought the end of the firearm down on Neil's head.

Neil felt the flare of pain for a split second before all went dark again.

∽

The pattering of rain on rock roused Neil back around to the world of the breathing.

He rolled onto his side, groaning as his body protested the shift.

Between the plane crash, the ambush, and the trip through the woods, his body was beat up and had had enough. He rubbed his wrists where they'd been bound, feeling the sting of roughed up skin. His leg muscles ached, his back tight and stiff.

He attempted to stand, but found the ceiling of the enclosure was low, which didn't allow him to straighten up to a full standing position.

His knees tolerated this position, but not for long, and as a wind whipped through the rocky cut out, Neil discovered he was nude. There was still enough daylight to allow himself to inspect most of his body. There were two big gouges taken out of his left ribs, but they were no longer bleeding. Whether from the crash or from an attack, he wasn't sure, but he could see the wounds were going to cause him difficulties in the future without any sort of care or treatment.

He made his way to the entrance of the cave, seeing a set of thick branches lashed together to act as a door to this prison. Beyond the bars, the trees blew and swayed from the wind, the rain hitting the rocks just beyond and lightly splashing his feet.

Neil went back to the wall and pulled himself against the furthest corner he could, wanting to get some rest before determining his next steps. *How could he get free? How far away was he from the plane?*

He leaned his head against the surface and before his eyes could close, spotted something on the rock.

Looking closer, he saw the surface of the stone wasn't as

smooth as he'd initially believed. He went back to the entrance and stretched his arm out as far as he could. Filling his cupped hand with rain, he carefully went back to the wall and used the water to splash the area, gasping as he saw the etchings come forward.

Neil, one said.

Tyler, said the other.

Sandra had been here.

5

———

Tyler stood patiently in the parking lot at the airport, waiting for the familiar sight of the small Cessna landing. It wasn't unheard of for the plane to be an hour late, the flight path varying depending on weather and turbulence. Dozens of times he'd watched it land, bumping and jostling as it made contact with the asphalt before it'd taxi across the tarmac to stop at the hangar.

But this felt different. Off, somehow. Looking at his cell phone he saw no missed calls, but with it approaching two hours since the plane was scheduled to land, his instincts told him this wasn't right.

He pushed himself off of his car and made his way towards the private terminal. He imagined asking the gate agent if they had any word from the plane, embarrassed when they would tell him it was landing in a few minutes. He'd laugh and return to the car, feeling like a fool. At least, that was what he hoped would happen.

Hopefully they'll have some answers, he thought, as he waited for an airport vehicle to drive by before jogging across the access road. He was glad to see some people milling around in the waiting area inside the hangar, a sign that they were expecting a plane to arrive momentarily. He was reaching for the door to pull it open when the familiar sounds of his ringtone began from his pocket.

Taking the phone out, he paused when he saw the number was his dad's work, his mouth immediately dry and his pulse racing.

"Hello?"

"Is this Tyler? Tyler Barton?"

The voice sounded familiar but Tyler couldn't place it.

"Yes. Who's this?"

"It's Mr. Adams."

"You're my dad's boss, right?" This wasn't good. His stomach dropped, his legs felt weak. He leaned against the glass window beside the hangar door for balance, sure he was about to topple over.

"Yes. Look, I'm sorry to be calling you, but we have a situation. We lost contact with the plane your dad was on near Ogre Peak. I'm calling, Tyler, because it's believed the plane has crashed. We've been unable to establish any radio contact with the pilot or the two passengers since that time. In fact, we've lost all contact with the plane. Even the emergency beacon. Where are you right now? I'd like to send someone to pick you up and bring you to the office so we can get a formal briefing with the police and Transport Canada."

Ogre Peak.

The mountain's name spun through his head like a hurricane.

Mom. Dad. Today.

Why did this have to happen again? On this day? At the same place? He was breathing heavier now, but the sound of the man's voice brought him back from the brink of a panic attack.

"Tyler! Listen, stay with me. I know this is a lot. I'm sorry to call you and tell you this over the phone. Where are you? I'll come get you personally."

"That's ok, sir. I'll get my grandpa to pick me up and we'll be at the office in an hour."

He hung up the phone before the man replied, already dialing his grandpa.

"Tyler, my boy! What's the word?"

"Grandpa. Dad's office just called. Actually his boss, Mr. Adams. Apparently... apparently dad's plane crashed near Ogre Peak. I'm at the airport waiting for dad, but dad's not coming. Can you come pick me up and bring me to dad's office? Please?"

He was in a trance. Shock was turning him robotic.

"You in the car, Tyler? Don't drive, hear me? Just sit in your car and don't do anything."

"I'm at the hangar, grandpa."

"Walk back to the car. I'll stay on the phone. You walking?"

"Yeah," he said, forcing his legs to move. He looked to make sure an airport luggage transporter didn't run him down when he crossed the access road.

"I'm at the car," he said, fumbling with the keys to unlock the door, completely forgetting about the key fob that would've unlocked the door with ease.

"Perfect. Tyler, you know better than anyone that your dad is a survivor. If that plane went down..." he didn't want to say *if Neil survived,* "Your dad has the one necessary tool in his toolbox every minute of every day to survive. You know what that is?"

"No," Tyler replied, his eyes blurry with tears.

"His brain. Even if the crash was rough, he can dress a wound, splint a break. He wouldn't panic. *You know that.* He'd assess his surroundings, assess his situation, and then make rational, calm, prudent decisions to make sure he would survive until rescue came."

"Yeah," Tyler replied, voice cracking.

"Don't panic, I'll be there in twenty minutes. I promise."

His grandpa hung up and Tyler pressed the button, locking the doors. He stared through the windshield, not bothering to turn on any music.

He sat in silence and waited for his grandpa.

Tyler watched as his grandpa pulled into the lot and parked two spots to his left. He got out and when his grandpa stepped out of his car, he stumbled to the man, arms wide. They embraced, his grandpa squeezing him tight and kissing his forehead.

"He'll be fine, Tyler. It's your dad."

Tyler gave a short nod, letting the security of his grandpa's hug relax him. They stepped away after a moment and walked to his grandpa's car. Thousands of scenarios ran through Tyler's mind as his grandpa left the lot, the airport, and before long accelerated and entered the highway that led back to the city. Tyler kept running the same thing over and over in his mind as they wound through the city streets and approached the skyscraper that housed the business offices his dad worked for. The date, the location. His mom. His dad. First her, now him. Over and over again, it played on a loop until his grandpa pulled into the parking lot of the building. They were met in the lobby by Mr. Adams' personal secretary, an older woman with a kind face. She escorted them to a private elevator without a word, entering an access code for them. She didn't join them in the elevator, instead leaving them alone and returning to the desk she'd been sitting at when they entered. The elevator ascended to the top floor, and when the two of them exited, they were greeted by a set of glass doors that looked into a massive boardroom. An impressive 'C' shaped desk filled the space. There were twenty chairs around the desk, but only four were occupied.

When they entered the boardroom, the man at the head of the desk stood and walked briskly over to Tyler and his grandpa.

"Tyler, sir," he acknowledged, extending his hand to each of them. "I'm Larry Adams."

They both nodded.

"Please, come sit," he said.

The two followed, sitting across from the other three men.

"Let's keep the introductions short here. This is Mr. Fincher, my Head of Legal, this is RCMP Liaison Officer Janson and this is Mr. Herman from Transport Canada."

They each smiled as they were introduced, which made Tyler angry. They shouldn't be smiling or happy. His dad was *missing*. He wasn't here to pick up a bonus on behalf of his dad.

"Mr. Herman, please fill them in."

The man shuffled a few papers, finding the one he was looking for to ensure what he shared was accurate, and began.

"At approximately fourteen hundred hours this after-noon an emergency beacon was automatically sent from the plane in question. This particular type of beacon will only go off if there is an explosion or a sudden impact. This beacon cannot be triggered by the pilot or passengers and will not go off due to turbulence or sudden pressurization losses. In other words, the plane needs to be hit by something or hit something for it to go off. We tracked a possible flight path after the beacon was activated and we believe the plane went down near Ogre Peak. Military satellite imagery shows a dark clouded area near where we suspect the plane to have crashed, and two sources confirm that the satellite imagery appears to show smoke. They also confirmed this 'smoke' wasn't present on the previous pass or images."

Tyler and his grandpa shared a look, the man reaching over and putting a hand on Tyler's arm.

"Has a search party been dispatched?" his grandpa asked, taking the lead.

"That's where there's an issue. Approximately seventeen years ago a hiker went missing in that area. During the subsequent search the military cordoned off a large section that is no longer accessible to civilians. Because of this, no search party has been sent and one won't be."

Mr. Adams cleared his throat getting Mr. Herman's attention.

"I'm sorry, Mr. Adams, did you have something add?"

"The hiker that went missing was Tyler's mom."

The air in the room deflated.

"Well fuck," Officer Janson said.

"Seriously?" Mr. Herman asked.

"Afraid so," Mr. Adams said.

"You couldn't've mentioned that before they sat down?"

"It's ok," Tyler said, his voice cracking.

"I'm so sorry. I had no idea. But the unfortunate fact remains, there's an area larger than Vancouver that is no longer accessible to civilians near Ogre Peak. We simply can't send a search and rescue crew into the area. Janson, you or Mr. Fincher want to speak on this?"

Fincher shuffled some papers, looking like he wished he was anywhere but in the boardroom.

"We've reached out to the military. In fact, Mr. Adams has personally called in some favors to speak to the higher ups. The fact is – we won't be able to access the area. And while this may all be a complete shock, we've taken the steps to draft a proposal, which if you'd just take a look, you'll find to be most generous."

Fincher slid the papers over to Tyler's grandpa, who looked at the summary lines, eyebrows rising, forehead furrowed.

"Proposal?" Tyler said.

"Mr. Adams and his company are prepared to pay you $10 million as grievance pay for the loss of your father. This is well and above what his life insurance payout would be, but all things considered, an official death certificate will be difficult to procure for a number of years. We wouldn't want you to suffer any financial hardships or loss of residency due to..." Adams, cleared his throat again, motioning for Fincher to stop talking.

"Wait, what?" Tyler said, standing.

"For all practical purposes, right now, we have to consider the facts and the prudent thing to do is to officially consider the three men as no longer alive."

"Are you serious?"

"Tyler. Unfortunately, yes," Officer Janson said. "The military will not give clearance to enter the space. If one was to ignore that order, they would be arrested and would be looking at life in prison, if not worse."

"This is such bullshit!" Tyler said, walking back to the

elevator, leaving his grandpa and the other men sitting somberly.

"I'm sorry, we had no idea his mom was the missing hiker."

"How could you? In fact, you probably don't even know that today's the anniversary of her disappearance. You can take that offer and shove it up your ass, Mr. Adams. With regards from Sandra and Neil Barton."

Fincher, Janson, and Herman all looked in shock at Mr. Adams, stunned to learn another detail he'd failed to share about the connections.

Tyler's grandpa went and joined Tyler while they waited for the elevator. When it opened, neither of them looked back at the men who remained seated.

As the elevator descended, neither of them said a word. Low piano music filled the silence. Tyler attempted once to put a name to the tune, but his anger flared and he put those thoughts to pasture. They walked to the car, Tyler focusing on the vehicles that whizzed by on the streets and the people who walked the sidewalks in innocent bliss. Getting in, Tyler felt the stinging arrival of tears, so he shifted his body in the seat, doing his best to not let his grandpa see that he was crying again.

The trip back to Neil and Tyler's house went by in the blink of an eye, Tyler wondering if maybe he'd drifted off to sleep on the ride home. When his grandpa parked in the driveway of the house, Tyler got out and began to walk towards the house, stopping only when his grandpa called for him.

"He's not dead, Tyler. You know that. I don't care what

those suits in that boardroom think or what they said. Neil is alive."

Tyler turned and went to his grandpa, stopping a few feet away.

"I'm going after him," he said

"I know."

"I'll find him."

"Maybe. And maybe you'll find what you've been wishing to find all of these years."

"Meaning?"

"Answers."

His grandpa stepped to him, giving him a hug, and once again kissed his forehead. When the hug finally ended, they both looked at the house, looked at Tyler's reality.

"Wish me luck?"

"You don't need luck," his grandpa said. "Neil gave you all the wisdom you'll ever need to survive. I have faith you'll find him. And if you don't, you'll be amongst them."

Tyler smiled at that.

He stood on the front step and watched as his grandpa backed out of the driveway and waved when the car drove away.

He'd need to start packing now, if he wanted to get an early start tomorrow. It was only then that he remembered his car was still at the airport.

He'd need to drive the old SUV parked in the garage instead.

6

Tyler knew the first step was to get prepared.

It would be an eight-hour drive from the Lower Mainland to Golden. He'd packed for hundreds of hiking trips over the years, so he knew it wouldn't take long to get organized. In fact, he had most of his gear already packed for the trip they had planned on taking in a few days. Now he just needed a few extra necessities.

But the one thing he hadn't prepared for was *where* he was going. The most efficient outdoorsmen were also the most prepared, and one thing Neil had hammered into Tyler since he could walk was the idea of knowing your area like the back of your hand.

If you want to survive the unsurvivable, you should be able to walk through the area with your eyes closed, like you can at night in the house with the lights turned off.

Tyler smiled at the sound of his dad's voice in his head, rattling off the piece of advice he'd told him over and over.

So, he fired up his laptop. He saw his bookmarks open on the top of the page; wilderness sites, cryptozoology sites and comic book news pages. He ignored those and searched

'Ogre Peak', then logged onto a few of the wilderness living forums his dad and Tyler frequented. While the search results were loading, he went and grabbed a bottle of water. When he came back, he went to the web search first, not expecting to find much information of real use for what he was about to do.

Scanning the first page he found the usual results; how to get to and from Golden, BC, a page showing a chalet he could rent near Golden that was only accessible via helicopter, and the basic mountain facts – weather would be cold at the summit and it was approximately 6,500 feet high. Nothing that stood out or unnerved Tyler.

It wasn't until the third and fourth pages of the search results that things of interest began to catch his eye.

"My trip to Ogre Peak and why I almost died." Tyler right clicked and opened the result in a new tab. Clicking the next page button, Tyler was surprised at the first result on page four. "The military is hiding something near Ogre Peak." This one was especially unsettling to Tyler after the meeting with Mr. Adams.

He went back to the forum page and scanned a few results, but once again it was one further down the page that got his attention; "Why does the military have Ogre Peak blurred out on maps?"

He clicked the link.

"Posted April 17th, 2003.

Hey gang, as you know I love going into remote lakes. Well, color me shocked when my wife and I were looking at hiking into Twin Lakes north of Golden. It's set right in-between Ogre Peak and Amiskwi Peak and I'd heard stories of the lake being pristine by my uncle who used to frequent the area in the 80's. Well, I ordered topographical maps from the government and a massive area including the two peaks, the lake and most of the mountains

were all blurry. No elevation data, nothing. Any idea what gives?
- posted by hairyhiker32"

Tyler scanned through the first few replies, seeing the usual comments that people would post. The first reply said it was because the government wanted to keep hairyhiker32 away from its weed. The second reply said it was probably due to land treaty issues between Indigenous people and the government. The third reply said that hairyhiker32 was probably just too stupid to read the map they provided, which prompted some good natured back and forth between the commenter and hairyhiker32.

It was the next reply that turned Tyler's blood cold.

"I'm not privy to all the details, but I am former Canadian Forces and can give you some insight into what occurred. On June 1st, 1990 a female hiker was reported as missing. The area she was in with her husband was in the process of being segmented from crown land into military-owned private land. Not something that happens very often, but think of areas such as the rumored Area 51 in Nevada. Similar protocol. Keep civilians out by any means possible. I was stationed, off the books, near Golden, BC, when they pulled the plug on the search for the woman, who had actually given birth right before disappearing. From what I heard over the wire - she was still alive but due to quarantine protocols, the military was not going to release her back in the general population. She'd seen something she wasn't supposed to see. So, take it or leave it, but for what it's worth, something is happening out in that area and I'd suggest you stay away and take your search for pristine waters elsewhere. - posted by offthegrid14"

His mom had been alive?

They'd been forced to abandon the search.

Tyler felt like he was going to puke.

He figured it would be no use to direct message offthegrid14. It had been years since they'd posted the comment, and from the profile information, they hadn't been on the site in almost the same amount of time.

What it did confirm to Tyler though, was that he needed to go after his dad. No matter what had happened in the past, it had only been a day since the plane went down and no one was searching. For the plane, or any survivors. If any of them were alive, Tyler was currently their only hope of being discovered.

He scrolled further down the replies, seeing most people call offthegrid14 crazy and a conspiracy theorist, but near the bottom of the page, Tyler spotted a reply that had a paperclip on the side. A paperclip meant an attachment and he hoped it would be something of benefit.

Clicking on the reply he found this;

"Posted August 7th, 2006.

Hey all, just came across this. I wanted to add some information here. I am currently an RCMP Officer in Golden, BC. Recently, Ogre Peak has been featured on some History Channel Shows regarding conspiracy theories and such. We've been doing our due diligence and trying to let local groups know a few truths to aid in safe hiking and safer conservation. The first thing I'd like to say is NO. No, there is no secret UFO base nor is there an alien runway for alien craft. While what is happening near Twin Lakes is top secret and well above my pay grade, the military has at times invited some of us members into the area to assist with their training missions. Which leads me to the second thing. The area IS frequently used for training and excursions. The Canadian Forces take their training seriously and they DO require untouched forested areas to be able to facilitate the training missions without concern of collateral damage IE civilian injuries or death. So, please, please stay out of the area. I have attached two pictures here for you. One is the approved hiking trails that do lead up to the secured land. If you use this map you will have no issues nor will you be arrested or have to deal with military members. Yes, there are military members that patrol and survey the area and border. The second picture was taken by local man Harry Dhesi. Harry and his family have lived in the area for most of their lives. This is a blurry picture of a military member with a high-powered rifle. Harry and his wife were hiking and stepped off the trail to take a picture. They were immediately questioned by a camouflaged member they didn't even know was there. This is serious and they shared this picture to let people know, this is no joke. They also shared it, because as you can see from the blurriness, this is the most probable cause of all of our Bigfoot sightings. Be safe. - posted by RCMP Officer Rich Carson."

Carson.

The last name rang a bell.

No? It couldn't be?

Tyler jumped out of his computer chair and went to the scrap book. Flipping it open to the June 3rd, 1990 newspaper clipping of his mom's disappearance he saw the name listed – *Officer Ron Carson.* Was that Rich's dad? It wasn't uncommon for kids to follow in their parent's footsteps, especially in small towns.

He clicked print on the attachment of the hiking trails, knowing this was a fortuitous piece of luck. He closed the browsers and decided to force down some dinner and finish packing.

Tomorrow would bring an early start, and while he knew his mind would be racing the entire drive, he wanted to try and calm himself and just focus on the task at hand. He needed to not forget anything. A distracted mind was a mind that would forget *something,* and that something could very well be the one piece of equipment that might save a hiker's life.

He tried to think of what his dad would be saying right

now, what pieces of advice or wisdom would be shared the night before a trip. Instead all he heard was his dad repeating over and over, *'come find me.'*

He tossed some Pizza Pops in the microwave, knowing they weren't the best option to eat, but he wasn't in the mood to make food from scratch. As he leaned against the kitchen counter, he looked into the living room. The first thing his eyes fell on was the picture of him and his dad hiking in Alaska.

They both had smiles on their faces as they stood before a lake bathed in the afternoon sun.

"I'm coming dad," he said, as the microwave beeped.

"I'm not giving up on you."

7

———

GOLDEN STAR, JUNE 2ND, 2007

DETAILS OF PLANE CRASH EMERGE.

Golden RCMP have released details on a small plane crash that occurred yesterday near Ogre Peak.

Officer Rich Carson stated that a hiker had radioed in that a small plane had looked to be in distress, but they stated the plane would have crashed in the secured military area.

The plane was confirmed to be an employee transport plane for Adams Mining and Surveying.

When reached for comment, owner Mr. Adams indicated that they had already contacted next of kin and that it was even more heartbreaking to believe all passengers on board had not survived. Mr. Adams also stated that it was devastating for one family in particular as it also happened to be the anniversary of another tragedy in the area almost twenty years ago.

Golden Star has confirmed that one of the presumed deceased onboard was Neil Barton, husband of Sandra Barton who went missing on June 1st, 1990 in the same area.

We will continue to monitor the story and provide updates when available.

8

———

MAY 31, 1990

They had watched the two hikers for days now. Always hidden in the shadows, camouflaged in the trees. The man and the woman had no idea they were being trailed, but from their observations it was clear this couple were experienced in the wilderness.

It probably helped that the woman was distracted.

They were both surprised the first day when they saw her protruding belly, and as their stay in the back country increased, they noted the number of times she grimaced and cradled her stomach; her pregnancy having come to term.

They radioed back to the higher-ups, asking what they should do, how were they supposed to approach this situation. Were the two needing to be eliminated and left for the scavengers to feast on, or were they to keep their distance and continue to watch? No clear answer was relayed at first, which made them uneasy. This was a finely tuned program, a machine that always connected the dots. No reply was unheard of.

At the midpoint of the day, the woman screamed and the

man went about starting a fire and boiling water. They radioed back – the woman had gone into labor, the child would be born any time now.

The voice on the other end told them to continue to observe and to be aware that a large predator had been frequenting the area, but their tracking beacon had recently stopped sending signals. That meant one of three things – it had gone underwater, it had died, or it had learned how to remove it from underneath its skin.

When the sounds of a newborn crying greeted the two observers, it made them smile. It wasn't often they were privileged to watch humans this long and not kill them, but to see the miracle of birth really did bring them joy.

The call came in just before dark. If one of them separated from the other they were under orders to take them.

Just after dark, the woman said she wanted to try and go pee, maybe clean up a bit at the nearby lake. The man nodded and cradled the small newborn, the child having been given the name Tyler. They left the man and child, following the naked woman as she traversed the path to the edge of the lake.

As soon as she stopped and sat delicately on a downed tree at the shoreline, they moved in. Unfortunately, she heard them approach, as just before the butt-end of the rifle was brought down on her head, she turned and shouted.

They picked up her limp body and hauled her into the trees, making it into the underbrush just as her husband rushed into view.

"Sandra? Sandra!"

They radioed back, noting that the man had heard a yell and came for his wife, but the baby was alone back at the campsite.

They were told to leave it and bring her to the enclosures. She'd be examined and it would be determined if she was of any use.

They left the man screaming her name, carrying the woman to her prison.

9

JUNE 2ND, 2007

THE CLANK OF A METAL PLATE BEING TOSSED INTO HIS CAGE startled Neil awake.

He shuffled over to the slop that was supposed to be his breakfast.

Better than nothing, he thought, as he shoveled some of the goop into his mouth with his hand. He didn't know if it was because he was so hungry or if the food was actually delicious, but he couldn't stop shoving it into his mouth. Before long he was licking the old camping plate clean. Once the plate was clear, he made sure to slurp up as much of the goop that'd spilled onto the cave floor as he could. A canteen was rolled into the cave moments after he slid the plate back out.

He unscrewed the cap and drank deeply, but this was where his wilderness training kicked in.

He took one big gulp, then a second smaller sip and let that sit in his mouth, feeling the liquid absorb into his lips, cheeks, and tongue. He put the lid back on the container and set it in the corner where he'd slept, far away from any prying hands that might attempt to take the water away from him. Water meant life, and he was going to do his damndest to conserve what he was given. Food was one thing. He could always find berries or bark to get some nutrients, but water could be near impossible to find during certain periods of the day. If it was too hot out, he'd need to be smart and not move too much. If it was too cold, he'd need to huddle up and prevent heat loss. Both of that meant he wouldn't be searching for water.

A gruff noise from outside caught his attention, so he made his way back to the bars. Looking through, he spotted two camouflaged men walking in the short valley below, both carrying firearms. What caused him to do a double take was the appearance of a massive brown bear behind them. It wasn't leashed or tethered. It was walking along with the men as though it was a trained dog.

Just what in the hell is going on here?

He slunk back to the corner, letting his fingers trace the two words he'd discovered carved into the wall.

He was certain he'd seen Sandra.

If he could figure out a way to get to her, to talk with her, maybe then he'd be able to make his escape.

He didn't believe she'd be coming with him, even if he tried.

Something about her, that his brain was preventing him from remembering, told him that it wasn't his wife who'd been missing for two decades.

No matter how much he wished it was.

10

<hr>

TYLER DEPARTED FROM THE HOUSE AT SIX IN THE MORNING, feeling the first rays of the morning sun fill him with promise. Looking at the darkened windows made him more motivated to find his dad. The house had long missed the presence of his mom, but without his dad... it would just be a structure without a family.

The old SUV fired up on the first attempt, which was another sign for Tyler. He couldn't remember the last time it had even left the garage. Normally his dad would have changed the oil first and checked a bunch of stuff, but there was no time for that. If the vehicle suffered some, too bad. It was serving the family a greater good.

Highway One leading out of the Lower Mainland was surprisingly bereft of traffic that morning. He knew in a few hours it would return to a normal gridlock, but by then he'd be far past any areas of concern, further east through the province.

Usually he'd be listening to music, singing along to whatever was playing. Not this morning. He was focused on the road while running scenarios through his head. The first was how he would be getting into the area without being spotted. He figured if he spent a few solid hours of surveillance near the border he would be able to locate a blind spot. Maybe, if the border was being watched via remote cameras, he could slip in under one or near one as it moved.

The more pressing concern that he needed to focus on was the '*what if.*' What if he made it to the plane and there were survivors? He knew that whether it was one survivor or all three, it would be a monumental task to get them back out, but that was always the risk you took when heading into the outback. The mountains were inhospitable areas, places that liked to chew humans up and spit them out. If Tyler arrived and found three injured passengers, no matter if one was his dad or not, he'd need to determine who had the best chance for survival. That may mean leaving one or two behind. If the choice came down to it, could he leave his dad to die if one of the others had better odds of living? His dad would tell him absolutely. Ensuring those with a chance of survival actually survived was one of his more prominent wilderness rules. But Tyler was still unsure about whether he could make that decision himself.

Driving by the highway exits to Hope, the sky opened. At least one benefit, if there was such a thing, of his father disappearing at the beginning of June was the temperatures would still be bearable. 20 Celsius instead of mid 30's. A month from now the area would be scorching hot, and the threat of forest fires would be extreme.

As the hours went by and he travelled closer and closer to his destination, Tyler realized just how silent the vehicle was without his dad. Usually they'd be discussing trail routes or life in general. They'd be laughing about something ridiculous his grandpa had done. They both watched a bit of sports, enough to have heated discussions about various players or coaching decisions. But now, driving by himself with the music turned low enough to be background noise, Tyler felt a loneliness he'd never prepared for, and one he wasn't about to accept.

He knew life as a one-parent existence, but to go down to a no-parent existence was unfathomable.

By nine, he'd pulled into a gas station in Kamloops, filling up the tank and grabbing some snacks for the road. The SUV didn't have the best fuel mileage, and he figured he'd need to stop one more time on the way, but for now this act of doing something so routine felt good.

It felt normal.

He tossed the grocery bag of junk he'd purchased on the passenger seat before returning inside. He used the washroom, not able to bring himself to look in the scratched mirror above the faded porcelain sink. Back in the vehicle, he opened a bag of chocolate-covered raisins before driving back onto the highway and making his way towards Salmon Arm. Depending on how this section went, he'd decide on stopping there for fuel or if he'd wait until Revelstoke. So far, traffic had remained light the entire drive and that's what he had been hoping for.

Thirty minutes outside of Kamloops he passed a number of semi-trucks long-hauling through the mountain passes. Ever since he was a young boy, he'd loved passing them. The semi-truck would be travelling up the steep incline at thirty kilometers an hour, while they'd whip by, passing it doing one hundred. It made him feel like the trucks were standing still, and even today he smiled as he soared past the fully loaded trucks.

As the road wound and snaked its way through the

mountains, the weight of what needed to be done settled onto his chest. He lowered the window, feeling the crisp air hit his face and neck. It would help to keep some of the anxiety from building.

As the road signs informed him he was inching closer to Salmon Arm, he took a look at the gas gauge and decided to continue on to Revelstoke.

It was only about an hour from Salmon Arm to Revelstoke, but the road between the two always made it feel longer. He grimaced slightly as he drove through Salmon Arm, wishing he'd decided to stop and sit at a gas station picnic table for a bit. The interior of the SUV had a heaviness to it, a weight that kept pushing against his body as though a supernatural entity was sharing the enormity of the task to come.

I'll stop in Revelstoke, he thought. *I'll sit and re-center. Fuel up.* By deciding it now, he wouldn't talk himself out of it. He turned the music up and let it transport him away from his current train of thought. A well-deserved distraction.

He didn't realize just how much his brain needed something to focus on, something to take his mind away from his dad and Ogre Peak. Before he knew it, he rounded the corner and was entering Revelstoke. The turnoff for the Galena Bay ferry welcomed him, but he drove straight and crossed the bridge. He guided the SUV into the first gas station on the right and pulled up to the pump. While he filled the tank, he looked back and spotted the ferry turnoff sign again.

It brought back a memory from five years ago, when his dad had taken him for a two-week trip. On one of the days, they'd made their way to Nakusp and then, crossing at Arrow Park on the cable ferry, they'd done a one-day ascent and descent of Saddle Back Mountain. They had stood at the base of the wood shack that had been built at the top of the mountain, looking at the Arrow Lakes on one side and Whatshan Lake on the other. They'd signed the log book in the shack and had a small lunch, just enjoying the views and each other's company.

It was the simple memories that stoked a fire in Tyler. It always hurt knowing he didn't have anything like that with his mom. All he had of her were photos and what his dad and grandpa had told him. He sat at the picnic table letting his eyes wander over the names and words carved into the wood top. He knew he needed to get back on the road, but it felt divine to be sitting outside, the cool mountain air carrying its different scents.

His legs finally listened to his head and he stood, shaking them out. Climbing back into the SUV, he sighed as he buckled up. The seat had grown to be one of the most uncomfortable things he'd ever sat on, but at least he was almost there. He pulled out onto the road, leaving the picnic table and those memories behind.

A winding road greeted him. He turned the music up again, singing along, trying to get himself excited for the journey ahead. Even though it was a 'search and rescue' mission, Tyler was the only searcher, and the closer he got to Golden, the smaller and weaker he felt.

The drive from Revelstoke to Golden went by in a blur. The lack of cars driving too slow and large trucks impeding his progress worked in his favor, but he questioned just how much of the road he'd actually seen as he made his way to Golden. The fastest ninety minutes of his life went by, and before he had even clued in as to where he was, he was pulling into a drive-through to get some coffee. Once he received his order, he drove to the farthest spot in the lot and parked. Tyler pulled out the map he'd printed off and looked at the logging road that would take him as close as he could before having to hike in.

Sipping his coffee, he figured it would be a forty-five minute drive to the section of land where people could park and another hour of hiking to the farthest spot on the loop before arriving at the border of the public land. Once there, he'd need to find a way around the cameras and surveillance. He poured the last third of the coffee onto the cement by his car. He'd never been a fan of the drink, but he needed a jolt of caffeine to help with the nerves. Tyler folded the map up and set it on the passenger seat. It was time to go.

A few minutes up the highway, he took the marked logging road turn-off and found himself on a poorly maintained dirt road. From the looks of the tire tracks it appeared to still be in active use. At each corner he slowed and ensured that he gave adequate room for any logging trucks that he may meet as they barreled down towards the highway.

Tyler kept an eye out for where he'd be parking the SUV. He almost missed it as he was driving up the road, the worn down area to his right appearing with no warning. The volume of cars having parked there over the years had turned the shoulder of the road into a de facto parking lot. He was the only vehicle when he pulled up, but as soon as he shut off the SUV and stepped out to stretch, a large black Suburban arrived and drove over by him. Pulling in beside the SUV, the driver shut off the engine, but remained hidden from view by the tinted window. Initially Tyler ignored its arrival, but when he heard the driver side door open and then close, he looked for the person.

Tyler kept stretching and was startled to see an RCMP

Officer come into view, the crunch of boots on the gravel appearing to be amplified as the Officer walked closer.

"Afternoon," the man said, nodding at Tyler.

"Sir," he replied, returning the nod.

"Heading out for an afternoon hike?"

"Yup."

"Anywhere specific? Sorry, I didn't get your name."

"Never gave it. Didn't get yours either, sir. My name's Tyler."

"Tyler Barton?"

Tyler felt some air deflate from his lungs.

"Uh, yeah."

"We were tipped off that you might be making your way up here."

Who the hell would have called? His grandpa? Mr. Adams?

"I'm Officer Carson. Rich Carson."

Tyler immediately recognized the name.

"Your dad searched for my mom. For like a day. I saw your post on the hiker's group."

"Yeah, my dad used to be RCMP. Sorry about your mom. Shit, sorry about your dad. But I'm here to tell you, you won't get into the area. You can try, sure, but they keep close tabs on the borders, and because of the plane crash, even more members have been spotted patrolling on the edge. I'm not going to stop you from enjoying a hike, but I am going to tell you that any hope of getting in there is useless."

"I appreciate the lecture. I'm just going for a hike. I want to try and get some closure and if I can't physically go to the area, I want to get at least as close as I can."

"I hear that."

"Am I free to go?"

"Yeah, you were never detained. Be safe, Tyler. These woods aren't like any woods you've ever been in."

They stared at each other for a moment, before Officer Carson returned to the Suburban. When he backed up he took a long look at Tyler then drove away. Tyler waited until the cop was gone, then shouldered his pack and started up the trail.

11

———

Every time Tyler came to a part in the trail where the trees didn't block the sky, he looked up to the blue above. It wasn't lost on him that his dad may be staring at the same sky, struggling to survive, waiting for rescue. If his dad had somehow survived the crash only to succumb to his wounds, he would've died probably looking up, up at the sky Tyler now gazed at. These morbid thoughts kept popping into his head, and each time they did it was harder and harder to think about something else.

If he was to make any progress and find a way into the protected area before night fall, he'd need to focus on his pacing and monitor his breathing. A big part of being able to do their hikes was conservation of energy expenditure. No matter how excited they were to go on a hike, they never rushed the start, making sure to keep their legs under them and never letting their packs feel heavy. His dad had said it so many times it was now a shared joke between them. Just when *would* Neil say '*check your pace?*'

Every thirty minutes he'd take a sip from his water bag that was attached to his pack. He'd swallow half and let the other half roll around his mouth before swallowing that. He made sure to not gorge himself on the cool fluid. Cramping was the last thing he needed to deal with.

The trail system was easy going and groomed. It was a far simpler hike than Tyler had expected, and he made short work of the distance. Coming up a long ascent, he spotted a small sign a dozen feet up in a tree. Taking out his single lens binocular, he focused the view on the sign until he could read what was printed on it.

Private property. All trespassers will be prosecuted. This area is under video surveillance and patrolled by armed security personnel.

From here, the trail curved off to the left in a semi-circle, running beside a dense line of trees that created a natural fence. This was where hikers were not supposed to cross.

He continued along the path, doing his best to act natural, knowing the cameras were watching. Tyler glanced around, trying to appear casual, as though he was looking at the trees or birds. In truth he was trying to find a perch or lookout where a soldier would be stationed. He also kept looking for where the surveillance cameras were placed.

It didn't take long before his due diligence paid off, first spotting two cameras pointing at the trail in opposite directions and about a half kilometer later, a deer blind where he was able to see sunglasses and a rifle pointed at him. He decided not to bring any attention his way by offering a wave. Instead, he adjusted his pack and continued walking down the trail as though he'd not seen the camouflaged person.

He'd walked another kilometer, figuring the deer blind had long sight lines, before he looped around, cutting through the middle of the wooded area. He kept his movements slow, trying not to alert any cameras to his presence.

Once he'd made it close enough to be able to make out the cameras and the trail, he stationed himself in the deeper grass. From here he faced the two cameras pointed at either direction of the trail and would remain out of view from the deer blind.

Though they were never avid hunters, Tyler and his dad did spend time tracking different animals, and when they'd gone on a two-month summer hike through the North West Territories, they'd hunted and trapped animals for food. A lot of the lessons Neil had taught Tyler that summer were now being put into practice. The biggest lesson was patience. Sometimes, nothing would happen for hours. So, Tyler sat at the base of a tree, backpack still in place, and bided his time. As dusk arrived, he caught movement on the trail and watched as two soldiers walked by, oblivious to his presence.

He watched as they did their perimeter check, sweeping the area. He heard them radio an 'all clear,' before continuing on their way. That had been the first perimeter check he'd witnessed while in hiding, which made him believe he'd have at least an hour before they'd make the loop and return to this section of the trail. The cameras never moved, didn't pivot, the small red dot flashing from the power source where they were affixed to the trees. He set his watch to a silent alarm and waited. After thirty minutes the watch vibrated and he stood.

Walking in a straight line, he stopped at the edge of the deep grass by the trail and crouched, taking his time to look through the grouping of trees that made up the perimeter. After fifteen minutes of assessing the area thoroughly, he was confident there was no guard stationed on the other side. Staying low, he made his way directly between the two cameras, staying below their lens space. Once he stepped between the two trees, he dropped to his knees and waited for an alarm to go off or any spotlights to pop on. When nothing happened, he started walking. He found a deer path and walked faster, wanting to put some distance between himself and the perimeter. He'd need to find a place to bed down for the night, but before that could happen he had to ensure he wasn't being followed.

The fear that had gripped him about crossing the perimeter was now gone. Lost in that thought, he almost yelled when he heard a noise to his right. Something moved through the trees, out of sight. Large. Dropping and looking, he caught a flicker of movement but then nothing. *Maybe a bird?*

The most peaceful moments were when Tyler was in the woods. His brain would slip into its hiker's zone; nothing but the sounds of the forest around him and the subtle crunching of his feet on the ground. If his dad was with him, their breathing would fall into sync within minutes and the two would move as one through nature.

Now, in this foreign and mysterious place, Tyler let his brain slide into that familiar zone, finding it comforting and centering. His hearing started to increase as the daylight dimmed then darkened. He was able to hear the familiar far off sounds of elk calling, and even a howl or two, but it was the weird grunts and roars that had him curious and perplexed. Those were sounds he'd never heard, and the closest thing he could relate them to were made-up noises created for dinosaur movies.

As those noises faded, a new sound announced itself and it was a sound that Tyler was happy to hear – moving water. Coming along the edge of the trees he spotted a slow-moving river. Crouching on one knee, he waited at the tree line, looking for any cameras or movement. Finding neither, he scrambled to the edge and filled his canteen and water pack.

The sun had now set behind the basin's edge, the mountains shielding it behind its rocky peaks. The valley grew dark rapidly.

Tyler returned to the seclusion of the trees. Heat sensor equipment would pick him up easier if he was out in the open and exposed. At least if he was in the trees someone may assume his heat signature was an animal if they weren't paying attention. He knew the general direction of Twin Lakes, so keeping shrouded in the tree growth he continued along, keeping the river near. He wanted to put himself in a position of advantage wherever he camped for the night. Having a natural structure to hide him from the elements would be ideal, but being close to fresh water was also a bonus.

Using his years of finding such a place led him to find a spot that would suit him perfectly. The location was made up of two trees close together. There was an old stump from a third tree between the two. Looking at the smooth surface of the stump, Tyler was certain it had been cut down. Not thinking much of the discovery of the cut tree, he stepped up on the stump and slipped his backpack off. Grabbing a small package from his bag, he pulled his camping hammock out and got to work, wrapping the nylon rope from one end around the tree and tightening it. Going around the other tree, he cinched the clasp tight, ensuring the hammock was lifted and that it would have enough tension in it to hold his weight and keep him in the air. Climbing onto it, he laid his pack under his head. From his thigh pocket in his pants he pulled out his camping blanket and, once unfolded, tucked it around his body. He decided not to eat that night, saving the single serving for another time.

Using a breathing technique that his dad had taught him when he was small enough to understand how to do it, he fell asleep shortly, the miles travelled that day finally able to catch up.

While he softly snored, something lumbered nearby, stopping to smell the air. It sensed a new presence in the area, but the thing didn't have a threatening smell. Moving closer, it found the figure wedged into something between two trees. The visitor to its territory had a pleasant aura, one that needed no further investigation. Not like the gun-carrying things it had encountered before. The creature carried on into the night, looking for somewhere of its own to curl up and go to sleep.

The next morning came quickly, but that was fine by Tyler. He slipped safely from his perch in the hammock, dropping onto the stump below. While he ate one of his pre-packed breakfast bars and sipped some water to help get the taste-less food down, he worked to undo the hammock from the trees and put it back into its case. He did the same with the blanket, and twenty minutes after waking he was ready to go.

On the drive out, he'd prepared himself to make it into Twin Lakes by lunch and if things went as planned, he'd be able to start scouting possible crash sites soon after. Tyler knew the chances of finding the crash site were slim, but from what he'd seen on the printouts before the men at Mr. Adams office covered them up, he believed he'd spotted a red X near Twin Lakes. He knew they'd not wanted him to see it, but when he stood in disgust over the proposal to forget his dad, he'd seen it and taken a mental picture.

Now, with the day just beginning, he found an animal trail and followed it, ensuring he stayed within a comfortable pace and looked at where he was putting his feet.

The forest had come alive, birds chirping and little animals scurrying around. Tyler was in his glory, loving how pristine and untouched this area was. He knew the Canadian Forces would be present somewhere around here, but so far, he hadn't spotted any sign of another human having been in these woods. *That's not true,* he told himself. *That stump had been cut.* He realized now it was too late to examine it any closer, having left it behind. If he'd not been so fatigued last night and feeling the need to get his hammock up as soon as possible, he might not have missed that detail.

The trees thinned momentarily and, making his way up a ridge, he looked out over the wilderness that greeted him. The green of trees travelled further than even his imagination could picture. It was nature in its greatest splendor.

Far off to the North, he could see the first of the two bodies of water that formed Twin Lakes. The second lake was off to the North East, just above it from where he stood. He estimated it would be another four hours of hiking to get from where he stood to the larger of the two lakes. He used his single lens binocular and scoped the area, not spotting any signs of a crash site. He did see something that caught his eye near the lake, possible movement, but even at maximum zoom, Tyler was unable to make out what it was. His gut told him it was a group of soldiers moving around, but it could also be a large gathering of deer. He'd need to wait and look again when he got closer.

The terrain through the area had so far been extremely

manageable, which Tyler was thankful for. It allowed him to cover the ground easily enough, and with minimal obstacles he wasn't being slowed down or having to climb over or under anything. The less chance of injury the better, especially when he had no way to call for help.

Surveying the area ahead, he decided the most efficient approach would be to loop around to the west side of the lake and come down directly at it heading east. There appeared to be enough dips and outcrops to keep him hidden. It wasn't a fool-proof plan, but he needed to remain unnoticed for as long as possible. With that much movement happening near the lake, he'd be wise to bide his time and take a careful approach.

He made his way along a ridge, weaving in and out of the trees. Finding a steep decline, Tyler decided to head down to the bottom of the hill and walk through the trees below him. It was along that stretch of shale and loose gravel that he first picked up the low hum. At first he believed it was his pulse, but once he stopped and felt a vibration, it became apparent that it was an external noise.

He stopped moving and listened, trying to discern the direction it was coming from. The hum came every two seconds, accompanied by the vibrating sensation in his body. It sounded like it was coming from further ahead.

Slowing his pace, he continued forwards, the hum gaining in volume. He made his way up a steep rocky section, his feet having to work to find a stable spot to put them. Once at the top, he poked his head over and located the source - a small shack. It sat twenty yards away, across a flat spot that looked manmade. The shack was built into the far side of the space, the hill continuing on above it.

From his position, Tyler spotted security cameras facing the front entrance, as well as iron posts around the perimeter. He assumed an electrified wire was attached to the posts creating a barrier for anything that came along unaware.

Not wanting to risk detection, or electrocution, Tyler moved back down the hill and hiked around the building, ensuring he stayed far enough away to not cause any noticeable disturbance or set any motion sensors off.

Once he no longer heard the hum or felt the vibration, he adjusted back to the original course he'd plotted and continued heading towards the western section of the valley. He was starting to get an itch to speed up and get to the lake as fast as possible, but he made sure to stick to his original plan and maintain this speed. Any mistake would be a costly one at this point.

Another hour went by as Tyler purposefully made his way through the woods. Catching an odd shadow in the corner of his left eye made him flinch and he came to realize that in the last few minutes, he'd begun to feel creeped out, as though he was being watched. He noticed that the sounds of animals had stopped, and as the sensation grew, he had the sudden urge to hole up in the base of an impressive tree. The wind had attempted to rip it from the ground, but the old roots had held firm, fighting back. In the aftermath, a hollow had been created where half the base of the tree had sunk into the forest floor a few feet. This allowed Tyler to hop over the dense roots and be shielded by three walls. The missing wall directly before him still offered camouflage, as the ground sloped up at an angle and another tree grew atop the mossy apex.

Noises came from further up behind the tree and after a few moments the sounds went from indistinct clatter to specific words. It was a group of people walking, all talking over one another. Tyler risked a look, and saw close to fifty soldiers in dark green camouflage fatigues marching. They were outfitted with packs and rifles, but what stood out the most was that they all had their faces covered by masks. Even more disturbing to him were the final ten members wearing gas masks. By the casualness of how they walked and talked, Tyler figured this was a group who believed they were alone and not being spied on. Not that they had any reason to suspect he was nearby. He ducked down after watching for a moment longer and decided to stay put until he was sure that it was safe to continue. They marched away from where he remained concealed, but even as they left, he could still hear their voices, although he was no longer able to hear what they were saying. He couldn't risk being discovered.

Knowing he was only a few hours from the lake made this wait excruciating. Soon, it became apparent that he wouldn't be moving any more that day. Only thirty minutes later the voices grew louder and the group returned. This time, Tyler's heart stopped when the man who he believed to be the commanding officer loudly announced that the group would take a rest break and stop to eat. Tyler huddled against the base of the tree as the soldiers started fires and began to eat. From where he was, it sounded like they were having a good time. Laughter continuously erupted and as the day stretched on, Tyler wondered if they were going to announce they'd be sleeping where they were as well. He should have been at the lake by now, but here he was, trapped by the tree, trapped because of the soldiers. Meanwhile, Tyler could only picture his father laying amongst the wreckage of the downed craft.

As the day continued and the sun started to lower in the sky, Tyler began to think about getting his camping blanket out. He heard the commander bark to the gathered men that it was time to carry on and that if they marched at a decent pace, they'd reach their barracks by dark.

Once again, Tyler waited patiently for the group to leave and, after another hour, decided it was safe for him to start a small fire. Where he had hid was fortuitous for a fire, as he was concealed in three directions, and the fourth had a decent enough barrier. His only concern would be the crackle of the burning wood, but he made a plan to have it burning just long enough to warm up some food packets and himself before he doused it for the night. The trees and lack of daylight would hide any smoke from searching eyes.

He gathered moss and dry deadfall and had a fire going in no time. The food was hot in moments, and he allowed the warmth to seep into his muscles just as fast. It was when he began to douse the flames with dirt that he caught a glimmer in the night.

Something, straight ahead of him flashed and moved, a brief illumination. It flashed again closer to his left.

He straightened up, reaching for his pack. Tyler didn't take his eyes from the forest in front of him, searching for more movement. He unzipped a side pocket and pulled out his foldable camping axe. With a flick, the axe became one solid unit and he stood, feeling emboldened with the tool in his hand.

The thing approaching must have taken his movement as a threat as suddenly the two glimmering orbs went from only a foot above the forest floor to a dozen feet in the blackened night.

Tyler inhaled sharply as he realized how immense the thing in front of him was. He glanced down, finding a piece of wood that was still burning on one side, but had an untouched half. Tyler grabbed the stick and heaved the burning spear towards it.

As the flame flew through the air, it outlined the shape of the creature, making Tyler's blood run cold. When the stick hit the ground and flames splashed towards it, the beast turned and fled, its sizable paws causing the ground to rumble.

How sleep was to come that night Tyler was unsure, but within an hour of the incident, he was curled up against the tree and dozing peacefully. Long through the night, the creature loomed in the periphery, curious about the small territorial intruder who'd frightened it off.

12

———

The events that occurred just before sleep played in an endless loop throughout Tyler's dreams.

He found those eyes in the dark and watched the beast approach. He replayed it over and over. Heaving that burning branch, the flame arcing high before landing with a splash of sparks before the creature. But in his dreams each loop changed, slightly different from reality.

In one, when the flames illuminated the beast, Tyler found he was looking at a stretched, elastic version of his dad, Neil having turned into a half-burned human that was elongated and floppy, as though his body was rubber without a skeleton to hold it up. As Neil walked towards his son, he screamed '*Tyler,*' over and over, his mouth growing longer with each shriek.

In another, the beast had its insides on the outside and as it roared at him, coarse, dark fur flew forth from its stomach. Its organs shivered and pulsed, stomach acid mixing with blood that pumped and splattered the forest floor.

While he slept, Tyler groaned and shifted, moving back and forth in the grip of this restless sleep.

A passing deer was spooked as it pranced by, not expecting another living soul to be anywhere near where it walked. But when Tyler moved and let out a pained noise, the deer sprinted off into the trees, leaving the source of the sound well behind.

The next morning, when Tyler finally rubbed his eyes and yawned wide, his spirits dampened. Sitting at the base of the tree in the woods, ashes marking where he'd had his fire, he felt defeated. He'd woke wishing it all had been a horrible dream; his mom, his dad, the plane and this place. But even as the morning dew clung to the plants and the mossy forest floor, he tried to hype himself up for the final push. He'd believed he would've already been at the lake by mid-afternoon yesterday. Now, only a few hours walk from his destination, he felt the determination and the resolve return.

He was going to find his dad.

Dead or alive.

Any hope of making it to the lake when he thought he would were quickly thrown to the wayside only an hour later. A large section of the forest had sloughed away creating a sheer cliff face and a drop of nearly a hundred feet. While the terrain until that point had been fairly flat, this created an impassable area. So, Tyler had to detour even further west, and it was along this section that he came across the three rivers. Each one snaked back and forth, the water moving at a fast-enough clip that he would struggle to keep his footing if he tried to wade across. Tyler guessed if he followed this back to the source, he'd come to a single, wider river, but with these three being so close together, he decided to try and find a narrow place to cross.

Following them further west, he found he was correct in his thinking, able to safely cross the first river, then able to repeat for the second and the third. When he'd finally made it to the other side of the three water barriers, he traversed an area of majestic boulders that had rained down from the hillside many years ago, before arriving at the summit of the furthest western bowl, overlooking the lakes. The wilderness wasn't overly hard to hike, but the constant setbacks and detours were beginning to wear on Tyler's psyche. It was at the top of this hill that he really felt despair. After doing some mental math, Tyler felt his stomach knot when he realized he was probably further from the possible plane crash location than he had been when he'd infiltrated the perimeter.

If he could've yelled, he would've, but from his location, he suspected the sound would echo out across the open space and would act as a targeting beacon.

While he was determining what to do next, his eyes picked up a dark shape moving near the edge of the lake. He didn't believe it was the thing that had approached him last night, but whatever it was – it was huge. Tyler struggled to comprehend just what could be moving down there that could be *that* size.

For now, it was neither here nor there. He couldn't see what it was and it was too far away to cause him any harm. He continued to make his way further north along the lip of the bowl, looking for a solid place to make his descent down to the flats at the bottom.

Another five kilometers north and Tyler came to a low growth clearing. This was the first sign he'd seen of human interference among the trees. Sure, he'd found that building and had hidden from the soldiers, but this area had been logged at some point. The way the trunks still had roots and were pushed aside and left on an angle suggested to him that it had been clear cut and a Bulldozer had come through after to remove the stumps.

He hustled across this space. This would be an easy area for someone with binoculars or a long-range scope on a rifle to spot movement and track him. He breathed out a sigh of relief when he entered the trees on the other side. He had no way of knowing if he'd been spotted, but if he had, they'd lose sight of him once he was hidden by the trees.

Looking at his watch, he was once again dismayed to see that time was slipping away. Tyler wanted to give himself a solid block of daylight to do a sweep and look for any signs of the crash, but he began to realize that it wouldn't be happening today. With the way his descent to the floor of the basin was slowed by the obstacles he kept encountering, he'd need to make it to the bottom of the bowl and then find a place to set up camp. The sun was dipping, and soon the shadows would creep along and overtake everything. The darkness of night was the only sure thing he could predict for the rest of the day.

After searching, Tyler found an old goat trail and followed it down the hill as far as he could before zigzagging back across the side until he came to a boggy section. His feet wanted to slip and slide underneath him, but he grabbed a broken branch and used it to steady himself. His stomach grumbled as he made it to the end of the muck and he smiled with the arrival on the floor of the valley. From the higher elevation, the bottom of the valley had appeared to be flat and would be easy to travel across.

Now, standing here, looking in the direction of the lakes, Tyler saw that it was far from the reality of what the wilderness was offering. The terrain was hilly and wavy and he'd be climbing up short ascents just as much as he'd be going down them. His heart hurt at the discovery, but he knew that he was once again that much closer to possibly finding his dad. It was these small moments of hope that he'd need to call upon to keep pushing forward.

Looking at his surroundings, Tyler began to search for a place that would keep him hidden for the night. The trees here were thicker than they'd been at the top of the basin, which allowed for him to find a place nestled between three thick cedars. Once situated in the nook the base of the trees created, he opened two food rations and ate them, pretending they had taste.

The quiet serenity of just one man lying on his back and enjoying the appearance of the stars in the sky filled Tyler with the joy that kept trying to be beaten down, bashed away. *He was close.* He knew he'd succeed.

As night arrived and the animals changed guard, the owls hooting and the bats flapping through the air, Tyler began to realize that there was another sound that was sharing the space reserved for the normal nocturnal residents. A sound that wasn't natural.

He focused, closing his eyes and concentrating on picking up the sound again.

It was very faint.

He turned his head to the left, but struggled to find it in the night's symphony. He was positive he heard it. Holding his breath he listened again.

There it was. *A beeping.*

Were his ears playing tricks on him?

He waited, holding his breath again.

There it was.

A beep. One beep every four seconds.

Getting to his feet, he waited until he was confident of the direction the sound was coming from, and started off towards it. With how utterly dark it was, Tyler had to take extra care while walking through the forest. He made sure his pack didn't get snagged on any branches or, even worse, if he was to trip on an unseen fallen tree. The forest floor was covered with roots that pushed through the soil, and mossy sections seemingly placed there so that someone would slip and fall.

Methodically moving through the night, Tyler would take a dozen steps then stop. Once he heard the beeping and knew he was on the right path he would take another dozen steps in that direction.

The closer he came, the more heightened his adrenalin.

Was it the plane's emergency transmitter? It could very well be it. Even if the suits in the boardroom had said no beacon was going off, Tyler knew he couldn't trust them.

Wanting to believe that it was coming from the downed plane, he continued. It was going to be a long shot to stumble upon the source in the darkness, but once again, Tyler summoned hope that this would reunite him with his dad.

He made his way another dozen steps as the beeping grew in volume. Two dozen more steps and it was as though someone had turned up the stereo system. The beeping reverberated all around him. If it grew any louder he'd need to cover his ears.

A strange flash caught his eye through the trees. Not a glimmer like the intruder from the night before, but an honest-to-god light. He stopped and dropped. It flashed through the trees again, and when it passed by Tyler, he rolled over and squinted. *Had it been a spotlight? Was there a person searching the woods for him?*

Crawling ahead, he could see where the trees thinned. Just beyond that was a clearing. Stranger still, the clearing had no grass on the ground, but was instead dirt and gravel.

Another reflection of light. The heat rush of adrenalin coursed through his body when he saw that in the middle of the clearing stood a pole, close to ten feet tall. A light was affixed to the top of the pole, which rotated around the clearing, illuminating the darkness along the periphery.

From where Tyler was crouched, he could see a box sitting on top of the light case. It was from that square that the sound of the beeping emanated. He remained behind the tree, staying low to the ground and watched, the light and the sound hypnotic, almost drawing him in.

Off to his left he noticed movement and, looking over, spotted a black bear lumbering through the trees. Something in the way the bear moved told Tyler that it was also transfixed by the pattern of beeps and flashes. Its eyes looked glossed over. It continued forward, passing Tyler close enough that he could've reached out and touched the brute, but it didn't even acknowledge that he was there.

Tyler stared as the bear approached the edge of the trees, stopping just before it entered the clearing. The beeps increased in frequency and the light flashed faster. Tyler became disoriented, as though he was trying to walk while a strobe light was going off. He watched with apprehension as the bear stepped out of the trees. It took two drunken steps into the clearing before all hell broke loose.

Massive spikes burst upwards from where they'd been hidden within the ground, impaling the beast. The spikes shot twenty feet into the air, eviscerating the animal. The force was so violent that strands of organs, muscle and hide flew far up into the night sky. Then without warning the spikes retracted into the ground, the remains of the bear sloshing into a puddle on the dirt. Moments later, a different sound began and it took Tyler a second to realize it was from the airborne parts raining back to the earth.

The sounds of the bear's paws and legs hitting the ground had barely ceased when Tyler saw a moose enter the far side of the clearing. He knew what was about to happen, but couldn't take his eyes from the animal. As with the bear, the moose was subjected to the same carnage as another set of thick, metal spikes erupted from below and made short work of the immense animal.

That was all Tyler could stomach.

He ran, leaving the beeping and the clearing behind.

As he rushed away into the darkness of the forest, he saw more animals walking towards the sound, all of them sharing the distant look the bear had as well.

Even from this distance he could hear the sounds of the spikes propelling towards the sky, the animals being speared through. Tyler kept running until he no longer could hear the beeping.

He only stopped when his legs screamed and his lungs burned. As he tried to come to terms with what he'd just witnessed, questions continued to flood his brain.

What was this place? Who was behind all of this? Why was he here?

He knew he needed to get some sleep, but it wasn't going to come easily. As more random animals passed by where he'd succumbed to exhaustion, he pulled his camping blanket over his head and focused on his breathing, the only thing he could currently control.

13

———

THE REST OF THE NIGHT WAS FILLED WITH BOUTS OF EXTREME terror bookended by frenzied anxiety.

Tyler remained huddled under a broken tree, allowing the branches pulled down by gravity to act as a shelter. He tried to calm down, but the second he felt as though he was settling, he'd swear he could hear the beeping again. Or he'd start to drift off to sleep, but several noises in a row would immediately return him to the edge of the clearing watching those poor animals be disemboweled and thrown sky high.

He was mentally done, traumatized, and feeling so alone that the sadness gnawed away at his marrow. It was an internal struggle between giving up and walking back to the area's perimeter, hoping to be discovered along the way, or just staying right where he was until starvation or the elements took him.

Memories of his dad floated through his brain as he rocked back and forth, but in his paranoid delirium, his mom also appeared in each and every remembrance.

He would see her smile from a distant shore, or she'd

wave from further up the hiking trail, but no matter what memory he brought forth to keep him motivated and returning his resolve to find Neil, he would be distracted by the vision of his mother.

Tyler didn't know how long he'd been sitting there staring at the base of the tree before he realized the sun was up and the birds were singing to each other.

The first graze of the sun's warm rays seemed to awaken his survival desire once again, and while his knees cracked and ached when he returned to a standing position, he hoisted his backpack and focused on the task ahead without a second thought.

It was those moments of extreme doubt that he'd battled through the previous night that he'd need to keep an eye on. The moments that could break your spirit always snuck up on a person, much like the desire to quit while running a marathon. He needed to be mentally strong, for he knew his body could handle the task. He pushed aside what he'd witnessed and focused on searching the area for the wreckage.

Tyler didn't know why, but he was now filled with absolute certainty that he'd find it.

That resolve was immediately put to the test.

The next thirty minutes became more and more frustrating as branches swatted at his face, roots tried to trip him up, and his pack seemingly caught on every tree he walked past. Tyler stopped and did another breathing technique his dad had taught him to re-center his energy. He let the air come into his lungs, held it, and then let it leave his lungs. While doing that, he would close his eyes on the inhale and open them on the exhale. He let the negative feelings leave, and soon he was ready to continue. Now, any barriers he encountered, be it rocks that were difficult to climb over, downed trees that forced him to go around, or marshy ground that slowed his progress, it no longer caused him to grow angry or lose his cool.

He was so focused on remaining calm that he soon realized he'd missed something in the surroundings. His nose had been trying to signal him. He stopped and inhaled.

There it was.

A scent *off* from the rest of the wilderness.

He slowed his pace and began to take more and more searching breaths, trying to discern what wasn't right.

A second scent, acrid and hostile.

Burning.

He checked the direction of the wind and found it was blowing towards him. He adjusted course and began to walk purposefully towards where he believed the smell originated. As he pulled himself up and over a thick slab of granite, the smell hit him again and this time it clicked.

Fuel.

It was similar to when they'd get onto a bush plane that had just been refueled.

Those two scents together were not good. What they represented was the worst-case scenario – the plane had crashed and burned. But Tyler still experienced a level of excitement, and it was growing as he walked. He was going to find the crash site.

Closure.

Something his dad never had with his mom. Something he'd never believed to have had for himself with his mom.

But if he did discover the plane crash and his dad was deceased, at the very least he had closure. Which was a hell of a lot more than he'd been offered in that boardroom with Mr. Adams.

He scanned the trees, looking for any sign of broken

branches or scorch marks. At first there was nothing, which wasn't unexpected. Continuing after the scent, Tyler looked for clues or signs. After another kilometer, he felt his heart sink when he saw the broken-off tree tops.

The air burned his lungs, the smell growing in intensity as he made his way up a steep hump of ground. Once he made it to the top he came to a stop.

The remains of the plane lay twisted and mangled, the charred cockpit resting haphazardly against the broken trunk of a tree.

Everything inside him told him to not walk, but he stepped into the debris field with thoughts of his dad at the front of his mind. Into the carnage, he casually inspected the pieces of metal and chunks of burned wood that led him towards the wreckage.

Sheered fragments of the shell of the plane scattered along the forest floor. Tyler saw large slash marks up in the trees where the plane had careened uncontrolled through the air, bouncing from one side to the other as it descended.

Arriving at the blackened husk of the former craft, he had to fan the air before him, trying to push the fuel-infused air from his face. He saw the wings were gone, unsure where they'd ended up, no sign of them.

He approached tentatively, bracing himself for the visual wretchedness that was sure to occur. If his father's body *was* in this charred vehicle, there was no chance he'd survived.

Trying to determine the best angle to get a look inside, he went around the tree that had stopped the front of the plane. Once around, Tyler heard a crackle and spotted a flicker. To his surprise there was still something burning within. He kneeled and saw low flames burning, which explained why the smells had made their way to him.

Peering through the busted side window, his eyes fell on

a burned body that was fused to the controls of the plane, a branch speared through their upper chest.

The pilot.

This discovery shouldn't bring anyone joy, but Tyler found a part of him *was* happy that it wasn't his dad. It also gave him the knowledge of what had happened to the pilot, which would bring closure to the deceased's family.

He continued around the plane, keeping his distance from the heat that still pushed from the wreckage. He examined everything, looking for anything out of place. It was on the third go around that he realized that only *one* body was in the wreckage.

Where were the other two?

Making another loop, Tyler tried to look at the surroundings with fresh eyes. There had to be something out of place, something different around the crash site that he'd missed. When he saw the boot prints heading off away from the plane, he cursed himself that he'd been fixated on the crashed plane itself. Inspecting them, it took him a second before it dawned on him that the person who'd made the prints must have been running, seeing the distance between each one.

Leaving the remains of the plane and pilot behind, he followed the boot prints, all the while trying to do some math. His rational mind needed to make sense of what he'd found so far, even if he was pushing the irrational aspects of where he was aside. One dead body still in the plane. One set of prints leading away. *Where was the other person? There were three confirmed people on the plane. Maybe they'd been ejected from the plane before it hit the ground?*

The trees abruptly ended, leaving him standing a short distance from a river. The sudden exposure to the world beyond the forest left him feeling naked and as though a classroom filled with kids were staring at him. That sensation left him when he saw the massive overturned stump. A twisted root system had been pulled from the ground when the tree it was attached to had fallen over, which now seemingly pointed towards Tyler. When he held a hand up to shield the sun, his mood changed and his heart jumped.

Gore and viscera.

Every single section of the root system was covered in splattered remains of something. Covering his mouth in revulsion, he stepped closer and saw that most of it was now dried and crusted, the flies that buzzed around appearing disinterested in even landing on it.

Was this the remains of the third body? Had they been ejected and impaled on this tree? Or had they made their way here only to die? If his dad believed it was the only option and he was the one that lived, could he eat a fellow human to stay alive? Tyler believed so.

A sharp sound off to his left startled him and caused him to stumble. As he caught his balance, his eyes discovered animal prints on the ground.

Something was very *off* about the prints.

It took everything in him not to scream.

14

———

They came for Neil during the night.

He was curled up in the back corner, shivering but dozing, when a noise caught his attention. But being so close to a dream state he wasn't sure if he'd heard it in his dreams or in the real world.

A denseness to the scraping sound reaffirmed it originated in the real world. He grudgingly opened his eyes as the cell door was pulled aside and two black-clad militia rushed him and covered him with a rough netting. They moved with such speed and precision that he had no time to defend himself or put up a struggle.

The net wrapped around him with synchronized movement, and before he knew it, he'd been tossed over the larger man's shoulder and they were making their way out of the rocky cell.

The moon was bright, illuminating the area around them. Neil couldn't make out much due to being slung over the soldier, but he could see enough to understand just how little of a chance there'd been of him escaping.

The trio descended a narrow path that had been cut into

the side of the mountain. Neil was startled to see them pass by more cells carved out of the rock wall, but in his gut, it made sense.

Who was in there? He wasn't sure, but not once did he see any movement, or any eyes shining with dismay over the sorrow of being incarcerated.

The other cages were a minor distraction to his real situation, and the uneven cobbled stairway soon returned his attention to his plight.

The nylon rope that made up the net was beginning to burn through his skin, the see-saw, back and forth action from each step causing more and more pain. The individual carrying him must have been in possession of a gun or a hard casing that had projectiles in it, as something jammed into his ribs and caused him trouble with each breath, as it hit his wounded side.

As they walked, spotlights flashed sporadically, and at one point he heard a hypnotic beeping. It was difficult for him to tell which direction it was coming from, but they travelled near the source, the volume growing in intensity before subsiding into the darkness. *Every four seconds,* he thought. *It beeps every four seconds.*

How long they walked, Neil was unsure. He was transferred from the initial carrier to the other individual at some point and when this happened, Neil made an effort to be positioned more comfortably, but it was to no avail.

The temperature increased noticeably as they made their way further down the side of the mountain. Newfound humidity made each inhalation a fight to not feel overcome by the extra pressure. *Just what was going on here?* From everything he'd seen so far, he'd known things weren't right in this place, but now, adding in the beeping, the other cages, things were becoming even more difficult to process.

A low rumble from ahead reclaimed his attention, and he nearly jumped out of his skin when a military-style jeep whipped past the trio, the two-militia saluting as it went by. Neil looked back to see the jeep and was surprised to see it towing a small trailer behind it.

While the jeep was black and the windows tinted and darkened, the trailer was open and Neil's view was unobstructed.

The trailer was filled with dead bodies.

But what petrified Neil to his core was the state of them. Some were covered with large gashes, some had appendages cut off, but the single constant between them all was obvious.

All of their legs had been removed.

15

Tyler couldn't take his eyes away from the ground. All around the root system the tracks told a story that was yet to reveal itself to him.

He was positive they were canine in shape and structure, but the size was unimaginable. Tyler knelt, placing his hand beside one of the tracks. With his fingers extended, the track dwarfed his hand. Noticing the tremble in his hand, he pulled it away, not wanting to accept how scared he was.

Neil had worked as a wolf spotter for many years for an oil company in the North West Territories, and would often share photos of some of the animals as they'd made their way near the oil sites. Tyler had even seen them in the wild, but never up close. He knew they grew large, but *this* large? Unheard of.

But would it be possible for a grey wolf to grow to immense proportions if it was the apex predator in a closed-off eco-system? Tyler didn't believe so, but for all he knew, maybe the Canadian Government was doing hybrid experiments. A grey wolf mixed with a malamute could theoretically produce a massive offspring, similar to when a lion and tiger mated.

The area was littered with numerous tracks that matched the giant canine prints. He also found several sets of human prints that appeared to be travelling with the animal who made the tracks. Neil's teaching had made Tyler adept at understanding the tracks were together based off the spacing and direction they travelled.

Tyler continued to follow the tracks, marveling at the size of the prints. No matter how scared they made him, they were majestic nonetheless. While looking at the tracks, something felt odd, and he stopped. Turning, he let his eyes wander over the disturbed riverside, and it took everything in him to remain calm and to just allow his mind to go blank while his retinas worked.

It clicked.

Someone had been dragged. That was the oddity to the boot marks. He'd not noticed it until looking at a long section of prints. He crouched and followed, seeing his hypothesis confirmed. Toe scuffs, drag marks, tread imprints. Someone had been trying to get their footing while being pulled along.

He returned to the beginning of the tracks.

Inspecting the set of boot prints closer, he discovered that they arrived here from the direction of the crash site. Crouching closer, he saw the telltale sole branding of the Oboz Bridger boots that his dad lived and died by. His dad had been wearing Oboz hiking boots for as long as Tyler remembered. Ever since he had an argument with a clerk at an outdoor store over a different boot's longevity, he'd switched and never went back.

He started to cry. Confirmation. His dad had survived the initial crash, his injuries minor enough to allow him to make his way from the plane to this spot. If the pilot had perished and burned in the crash, it meant the gore on the roots must belong to the third passenger on the plane. The Oboz prints painted a picture for Tyler, one that answered a number of questions.

Going back to where his dad's prints had changed from standing to dragging, Tyler noticed a darkened patch on some rocks. Blood. Another set of prints approached this spot and stopped, before changing course and following along beside the drag marks. Tyler connected the dots, and believed his dad had been struck on the head and dragged away. Disoriented, he would've been trying to get his feet under him as he was pulled along. Was this just his mind creating a story? Or was this what actually happened?

Dread coursed through Tyler. Had they dragged him down the river only to finish the deed and leave his body to rot? Would he stumble upon Neil's remains? Once again his gut instinct was to not continue, to turn and flee, but he had to know. He'd come too far. Twin Lakes was no longer his destination. He'd found a sign and would see where it took him.

At the point where the tracks disappeared into the trees, Tyler spotted something reflecting off the forest floor.

He smiled once he realized what it was.

Reaching down, he plucked his dad's Garmin watch from the ground. The straps were covered in dirt and the face was scratched, but after using his shirt to clean it off and wipe the front clear, he saw it was still operational.

His dad had known he would come for him. With a smile on his face, Tyler wrapped it around his wrist and threaded the clasp in place, feeling it sit comfortably beside his own watch.

He was more confident than ever that he would find his dad.

Tyler entered the trees, leaving the crash site and river behind. The trees were thicker and denser than those he'd already travelled through, but he pushed that aside. With thoughts of finding Neil at the forefront, he couldn't help but hope.

16

———————

TEN KILOMETERS OF HARD HIKING. TEN KILOMETERS OF backtracking and making sure he was still following the tracks and hadn't absently wandered off in the wrong direction. Ten kilometers was all Tyler had left in the tank before his legs felt like mush and he had to sit. The burst of hope he'd felt when he'd found his dad's watch had provided him with enough energy to keep going for the rest of the afternoon. But the number of days with low calories, low rest, and the excessive mileage on his legs had finally caught up with him. He was at the point of needing a rest before he would be forced to stop due to sheer exhaustion. It pained him to admit this, but he knew it was the smart decision based on circumstance.

A natural overhang near a pond would offer him some shade and shelter, enough that he decided to set up camp and start a fire. He could enjoy a hot meal, relax, and then build a lean-to that would keep him out of the night winds and away from the searching eyes of nocturnal hunters. The memory of that immense beast that had approached the fire was still fresh in his mind.

Once the fire had the water boiling, Tyler collected some wind-blown trees. He made quick work of them, chopping them into usable lengths. He notched the tops so that he could lean them against the overhang. This worked to create a wall. His wind shield was now in place and, taking a look from fifty yards away, he was delighted to see that the structure didn't look out of place if someone or something were to walk by.

With darkness approaching, he stripped down and waded into the pond. The water was glacial, and it bit his skin with an intensity only water that temperature can, but he let his body acclimate, and before he could talk himself out of it, submerged completely under, relishing the feeling of washing some of the grime and sweat from his skin.

If not for *why* he was here, this moment would be perfect. One that he'd think about for the rest of his life. Bathing in a pond, in a place where almost no human had ever been before. Tyler dunked himself again, letting the water cleanse his weary bones, before returning to the shelter. Once he'd drip-dried enough with the help of the fire, he re-dressed. Sitting, Tyler took the camping pot and set it between his legs. Spooning some out, he first blew on the fluid before slurping it in and enjoying the warmth that enveloped his body. The soup he'd warmed up seemed to work its way down his throat, into his stomach and then travelled to the very ends of each finger and toe.

As the sun set, Tyler felt content. He had felt like he'd overused the idea of 'hope' already, but right now, right at this moment of this journey, hope was the most accurate word to truly define what this structure and the food had returned to him.

He unfolded the blanket and laid his head on the pack.

A smile remained on his face as he settled in and shifted

on the ground to find a comfortable position. Even though he was exhausted, sleep was struggling to come. As he started to drift off, the sounds of something bashing through the underbrush arrived. Tyler sat and blocked the brightness of the still burning flames with one hand, peering into the dark beyond. It was in the darkness of the forest that the shape of the brute emerged.

This time, the behemoth was emboldened with a desire of its own.

Hunger.

17

———

THE RUSH OF THE BEAST CAUGHT TYLER OFF GUARD. HIS HAND had just covered the glow of the flames when it charged, his eyes adjusting in time to see the blackness grow blacker. The brute burst through the night and roared across the fire, landing with a thunderous impact beside Tyler.

He pushed himself backwards, putting some distance between himself and the thick paw that swiped through the air, narrowly missing a connecting blow with his chin. Tyler scrambled, back-peddling, pulling himself along with his hands while kicking the ground. His heels kept slipping, not able to get any traction. The mossy top layer slid easily off the dirt below, making Tyler feel like he was trying to crab walk across ice. The creature turned sideways, sizing him up, determining its next move. It was going to attack at the point of weakness, Tyler knew, so he tried to stay facing the animal, not wanting to expose anything that would elicit a lunge.

He rolled to his knees, circling the fire, putting the flames between the two of them. His new position was unsettling, exposing his back to whatever else might be lurking in the dark woods behind, but it was necessary for the threat in front of him. It was an odd spot to find himself in, but he tried to ignore the growing sensation of an ambush from behind.

Tyler backed away from the fire. First one step. Then another. Now steadied, he stood, raising his arms to appear as tall and wide as possible. If the creature could have, it would have scoffed at the display. While Tyler was 6'2, he wasn't a large man by any stretch. The creature probably weighed five times as much as he did, and if it decided to imitate him and raise its paws, it would loom over him by a solid four feet. But it was enough to flash hesitation at the display, enough to embolden Tyler and not let him feel as small and insignificant as he was when compared to the creature.

Man and beast began the dance of expectation and boundaries.

Tyler knew that the creature was waiting for an opening. The creature understood that Tyler was trying not to let a space open for that to happen. It was the same tango between predator and prey that had been happening since the Earth spewed forth its inhabitants. One would live, one would die, and the cycle would be complete and begin all over again.

A breaking branch and a gruff bark from off in the trees forced both combatants' hands. It was a case of itchy trigger fingers. As soon as the snap happened and the bark sounded, Tyler grabbed his axe from beside the fire and turned, swinging with all of his might. He'd been circling around, trying to get close enough to grab it, and the timing couldn't have been better. At the same moment, the beast lunged, coming across the fire as though it was not even there. The collision sent both of them sprawling, Tyler pinned between a tree stump and the animal. He waited for the onslaught of claws, teeth and pain to occur, eyes closed and chin tucked, but instead he was surprised when silence greeted him.

Opening his eyes, Tyler realized the creature was lying motionless atop him. No visible expansion of the ribcage, no thrum of a heartbeat.

Tyler wiggled and writhed until he was able to scurry out from underneath the mass of the animal. Rounding to the front of the beast, he saw that his axe blow couldn't have been more perfectly placed.

It was embedded deep between the bruin's eyes, pulpy fluid pooling around the shining blade. Its tongue hung from one side of its jaw.

Tyler had somehow defeated this beast.

Even with the fear of what was to come lingering, this victory filled him with further levels of resolve. He could do this. Nothing was going to stop him or come between him and finding his dad.

Off in the woods, hidden in the shadows, the immense shape watched the human slay the beast. It had played a small role in the event, but it still felt the warmth of joy.

Moving deeper into the woods, it didn't make a noise, as though it travelled on the wind and through the trees.

18

———

NEIL CAME TO IN A ROOM THAT WAS SO BRIGHT HE COULDN'T open his eyes.

He wasn't outside anymore, that he knew immediately.

His hands moved across the surface where he sat, finding it flat and smooth.

Man-made.

The smoothness of the floor and the smell of disinfectant rang bells far off in the back of his mind. It came through the fog slowly, but it finally clicked. He was in a lab. He'd be caged of course, imprisoned, but at least he was no longer at the mercy of the elements. He was still nude, but the room was considerably warmer than the rock cell had been.

Crawling, he made his way to a corner, feeling exposed due to the lack of vision. He had no way of knowing if this was close to the entrance or not, but it felt more comforting to have two solid surfaces against him than when he'd been sitting alone in the center.

While he thought through his next steps, he heard the buzz of a fan kick on from the ceiling. He thought it came from the far corner across the room from him, but he wasn't completely sure. What he was sure of was the air that now flowed through the room felt immeasurably divine, like a cold drink on a scorching hot day. His skin reacted, and he had a moment of peace. His nostrils detected a scent lingering underneath the freshness of the air.

It was a smell that transported him across time and space. It took him from that room to the tarmac of the Salluit Airport in Northern Quebec.

Neil breathed in deep and remembered the best day of his life.

Sandra and Neil had made their way back into Salluit after backpacking through the inhospitable forests surrounding it for two weeks. Normally these hikes were *their* time, a time to connect, a place to *be* with one another.

Instead, what had transpired were two weeks of constant bickering. Arguments about inconsequential things. Each day they woke with a glare towards the other. They stopped talking almost entirely, save for the occasional curt words to determine direction and what they were going to eat.

They'd planned on being gone for a month, but at the one-week mark they'd lashed out at each other, yelling, screaming and crying. Sandra suggested they turn around and return to Salluit, fly home. They'd reached the point where they didn't want to be around each other, out in the place that had usually given them peace and calm. There was no discussion of *after*. Nothing about what would happen once home, once back to the real world.

Neil had softened on the hike back. *Was this it? The end?* He loved Sandra with every fiber of his being, but they'd exploded. *And for why?* He didn't know. For whatever reason, the trip had morphed into two angry people in the trees, instead of two people who loved each other enjoying nature.

When they got to the airport, they were told they'd have a three hour wait. Since their arrival was unexpected, a plane would need to be flown in and, once it'd landed and refueled, they'd be able to head out. Hearing the details, Sandra had stayed leaning against the wall inside, while Neil went and sat on the rickety wooden bench out front. The dusty, dirt runway disappeared off before him, the first segment of the two-day trip back to the West Coast.

He took in the panoramic view, enjoying the lack of tall buildings blocking the mountains. Sandra came over and joined him. Even after what'd happened on the hike her presence beside him made his day infinitely better.

She placed a hand delicately on his, he looked at her.

"Can we talk?" she asked. "Legitimately talk. No raising of voices, no anger?"

"I'd like that," he replied, not sure what to expect.

"Why did we get like that? Why did everything boil over?"

She looked at him as he digested her question, searched his eyes for something that would speak to her beyond words.

"I don't know, honey. I don't. It was as though from day one we just didn't click on this hike. Normally, we're so in-sync with each other, but not this time."

She nodded, squeezing his hand.

"I have some news to share. I was going to tell you when we made it to our half-way point. I figured it was fitting to tell you in the woods, in the middle of nowhere, but I want you to know now."

His stomach lurched. He was going to puke if she said she was leaving him.

"Neil, I'm pregnant."

He stood, running his hands through his hair, then walked in a circle looking around, looking at her.

"Are you sure?"

"Yes. Confirmed. Due date is end of May, maybe early June if the wee one decides to not want to come out."

Neil was crying now. He went to her, hugged her, pulled her tight.

"This is amazing," he said into her ear, kissing her hair, her forehead, her lips. "I'm going to be a dad! And you a mom! We're having a baby," he said, practically jumping.

He knelt, putting his hands on her sides, then kissed her belly through her shirt.

"When we get back, we'll schedule an appointment to see what we're having."

"We can find that out?"

"Yes, Neil. Science lets us do some pretty cool stuff, you know," she replied sarcastically.

Neil remembered smiling after that. A lot.

They sat, huddled together, the irritation that they'd experienced on the hike long gone. When the plane was gassed and ready to go, they boarded.

As the small craft sped down the runway, the plane bouncing and jostling, Neil returned to the present. The smell of the crisp Quebec air was replaced when the fan clicked off and the brightness of the lights in the room returned.

19

———————

THE NEXT MORNING TYLER WAS PLEASED TO WAKE UP STILL possessing the renewed vigor from the previous night's battle.

He'd left the carcass of the beast for the forest to take back, to use what it needed. Other animals would come and scavenge, and as it rotted, it would return to the soil.

Without the lake as his main destination, Tyler confidently followed the trail that snaked through the trees. He knew to keep his alarms up, his senses high. If something or someone had taken his father, he didn't want to stumble onto anything unexpectedly. It wouldn't do them any good if they were both imprisoned or worse, dead. Tyler suspected his dad, if still alive, was with the same group as the military members he'd spotted before. He hoped to find them, to follow them back to their complex. He'd surveyed the area several times already from higher vantage points, but saw nothing. He didn't understand how a complex like that could be so well hidden, but Tyler knew the military would go above and beyond to prevent any of their secrets from being discovered.

This section of the valley was slow going. The morning had started out with an easy path winding through the trees, but now Tyler was encountering numerous down falls and broken trees. This area was mainly older growth, which meant that many of the trees didn't stand a chance during harder and heavier windstorms.

Due to this, Tyler kept having to tackle each new barrier individually. Over the last three hours, Tyler had covered less than a mile, and his frustrations were beginning to rise. Each downed tree meant he'd need to crawl under or over it, only to find another downed tree which forced him to stop and determine how to get past this new obstacle.

After climbing over a splinted trunk, he needed a rest. He drank some water, leaning against a still standing larch. His emotions needed to settle. He was no use to himself if he kept losing his temper, and the last thing he needed was clouded judgement leading to an accident and injury.

Wiping the sweat from his forehead, Tyler decided to sit for a minute, wanting his legs to stop feeling like rubber. Directly in front of him was another downed tree, which he climbed over. Another broken tree greeted him, but at least here was a stump that offered a spot for him to sit. His knees ached as he let his butt drop, but once off his feet, his body relaxed. He nibbled on some bark he'd peeled off, using it to clean the grime from his teeth. Looking around, he found this position allowed for a fresh perspective. Tyler enjoyed another mouthful of water, staring at a place in the trees that looked odd, though he couldn't figure out why. The green was a different green, lighter or faded. Then it dawned on him. It was the thinning of trees. The edge of the forest. It was still an hour's walk from where he sat but he couldn't contain a smile. With no one to share his excitement with, smiling was the only alternative, the only way for his body to feel that emotional change. He was closer. Almost out of this hell that he'd needed to cross. With any luck, there'd be a river or a clearing beyond, something to let him speed up and cover more ground while also allowing some energy conservation. This last section had left him completely spent.

Tyler suspected his father hadn't come through this area, certain that whoever had him had moved through the forest further up and he'd find their tracks on the far side. He'd diverged when it became too steep for him to climb without any aid. This route was supposed to be a short cut. It had been anything but, and not knowing how far ahead the kidnappers were, he was loathing the slowdown and delay.

Standing, he started off towards the thinning of trees. Thankfully, the short respite had refreshed his legs, and his arms no longer felt like jelly hanging from his shoulders.

Under, over, around, repeat.

Under, over, around, repeat.

It became his mantra, something for him to focus on and hold in front of his eyes each time a broken branch poked him or an unseen rock threatened to twist his ankle.

Arriving at the far side, he turned and looked at the gauntlet of broken trees he'd traversed and gave them two middle fingers held high. With the smile still on his face, he wormed through the thinned line of trees that acted as the border for the edge of this area. Stepping out from them he was elated at what he found.

A river.

Thirty feet across and moving at a fair clip, Tyler wasn't worried. It looked shallow enough that it could be carefully crossed, but he'd need to decide if he wanted to remove his boots and socks and roll up his pant legs or just let them get wet and deal with the probable blisters that would form later on.

He decided to hold off from making that decision and explore the area to his left and right. Tyler searched the river's edge, excited when he came across the tracks, recognizing the tread print of his father's boots again. The old man was still alive, at least at this point in their journey.

From off to his left, a bellow erupted across the landscape. Birds scattered and small animals dashed away through the underbrush of the trees.

Tyler was paralyzed with fear. The sound had vibrated through his bones, cementing his boots to the muddy ground.

A second bellow came from off in the distance, which Tyler recognized as an answer.

Tyler heard crashing and splashing and forced himself to look but he was already too late. All that he managed to catch was the trees on the far side moving and swaying from the force of whatever had pushed through them.

He counted to sixty before regaining the nerve to walk towards that area.

Once again Tyler was gob smacked by tracks in the dirt. They were over a foot long and a foot wide. The print was circular in shape and it reminded him of a large animal he'd seen years ago. On several safaris Neil had taken them on, they had witnessed elephants in the wild. They'd even tracked some for miles following their pad imprints. But this was different. Elephants had four nails that made clear, distinct marks. This print had a fifth. On the inside, medial aspect of the impression.

Another bellow sounded from some distance, but Tyler's

head snapped up as though the offender were directly beside him. When he looked across the river, more trees swayed as something trampled away, further into the woods, heading in the same direction he needed to walk.

20

———

Further into the wilderness towards an unknown destination he walked. He thought of his friends who'd have written their last exams by now, who'd already started summer jobs. Those who'd wondered where he was and why Tyler had missed the exam. Some would've already started packing, thoughts on their first year of University looming.

Tyler continued on, scared, frightened, but emboldened. Something kept telling him to keep going, that he was getting closer. But what? He wasn't certain, but a nagging thought had begun to form. Something in his mind had connected the dots and was forming the hypothesis that this animal that had bellowed and bashed through the woods was trying to aid him, guide him. A few times, he'd found himself at a place where he was uncertain where to go. Each time the animal would find some way of getting Tyler to move in the correct direction. That first time, distracting the beast by the fire had seemed random. But now, this bellow, it seemed more specific and Tyler was certain it was the same creature both times.

If this was the case, Tyler was thankful. If not, he was worried. It could very well be the beginnings of a delusion brought on by exhaustion and isolation, but he didn't want to dwell on that. The one thing he was certain of was that he hoped the creature kept its distance.

For the first time in days, Tyler could see darkened clouds coming into view over the far edge of the basin. The day was getting away from him again, the morning lost to the gauntlet of obstacles he'd had to traverse. Watching the storm gather, he tried to estimate how much time he'd have before the clouds were over him. He decided it was best to keep an eye out for a place to take shelter, but he wanted to try to put more miles under his feet. Tyler needed to remember that the mountain weather could change in a matter of minutes.

His mind was so focused on the potential storm and how it would slow down his tracking that he didn't even realize what he was now walking on.

An old road.

How had he not seen the signs? The path he thought he was following was six feet wide, with two narrower packed lines that would've been where the wheels drove on each side and short growth in the middle. It hadn't been used or maintained in years, but it was absolutely a road. This would make hiking a thousand times easier. Another excited thought popped into his head. This would lead somewhere. The end of this road may very well be exactly where he needed to go. He practically skipped as he started off down the forgotten road. The trees were thin and not as packed here, letting more natural light make its way to the ground than previous areas. Even with the dark clouds rolling in, the overall illumination of not being under dense branches gave Tyler an extra kick. If he'd not been hiking in a known hospitable place, he might've even started humming or singing a song, his mood had brightened so much. It soured slightly when he arrived at a place where another road that was no longer used crossed over his current one.

He looked in either direction, but nothing stood out suggesting he take that path. Tyler asked himself which way would be the most likely direction he should go, but he'd hardly had time to finish the thought when far off to his right, his mystery guide let out a call. It may have been muffled from the miles it had to travel, but it was enough.

Tyler didn't give it a second thought. If the creature wanted him to follow it this badly, then he was going to keep putting his faith in its calls.

This was the easiest section Tyler had encountered since before he'd crossed over the perimeter. He was bordering on running before he realized it, and eased the pace back to a walk. His excitement was getting the best of him. This was a common occurrence on longer hikes. You'd have two or three small moments of joy while experiencing extreme mental breakdown from the aches, the miles and the boredom. You'd get some sun and a meal in you and on a straight stretch you'd almost be full sprinting before you realized it.

He focused on his breathing, bringing it back in step with his pace, until he was calm and his stride was smooth.

As had happened several times now, his focus almost caused him to miss seeing something else of importance. It was a rock that brought his attention to the hunk of metal. Tyler stumbled on the rock and spotted the wreckage wrapped up in old growth just off the road as he caught his balance.

Upon closer inspection, it looked to be the rusted remains of an old military Jeep.

He unclipped his axe, *his trusty-beast-killing axe*, and started chopping the branches and small trees from the vehicle. Once he'd cleared it and could really see it, he was surprised that it'd been left to decay. *Maybe the engine died,* he thought, as he circled it. It wasn't until he came to the passenger side that he saw the damage it had sustained.

The tires were flattened from years of disuse on the driver side, the rubber cracked and broken. However, Tyler found the passenger side tires had been shredded. Running horizontally across the side of the jeep were four thick slash marks, as though massive claws had ravaged the vehicle as it drove. On the driver side, Tyler was still able to make out the faded writing, which read, 'Canadian Armed Forces.'

The roll bars on the jeep had been crushed downward. This would've taken an impressive force to cause, the coating around the metal cracked and flaked away. The material of the seats had long since rotted, the rusty springs left behind as a reminder of the shape that was once there.

The entire vehicle gave Tyler the creeps, as though he'd discovered a ghost ship in a harbor. He started to leave the metal skeleton behind when something off to the side caught his attention. Walking over, he saw that the white glint he'd caught was human bone.

He suspected that it was most likely a passenger from the destroyed vehicle, but he no longer cared to try and confirm it or even look for other remains. He needed to continue on.

The longer he stayed near this hunk of metal, the darker the woods around him became.

21

WHILE THIS NEW ABANDONED ROAD PROVIDED TYLER WITH AN easier path through the wilderness, its immediate drawback was how exposed it left him feeling.

He wasn't sure if this trail was monitored, but every sound made him cringe and duck, which, in turn, turned into a tremendous amount of time spent stopping and waiting. Night was approaching, and with the short distance Tyler had travelled since discovering the Jeep, he began the familiar task of seeking a place to sleep. *Just how many nights had he spent in this place?* He was already losing track.

Looking for a good crevice or overhang to utilize, Tyler searched the area, cursing to himself that the trees didn't allow for a clearer view of the hills beside him.

Twenty minutes of searching went by, the afternoon light dimming into the evening remains before darkness crept in. He told himself he shouldn't be feeling anxious. He'd find somewhere, but the longer he was in this strange valley, the less time he wanted to spend a night without the comfort of four walls and a roof over his head. As though the trees had been listening to his thoughts, they thinned off to his right, and he noticed an old wooden structure halfway up the hill. Even from here it looked abandoned, but Tyler couldn't be sure.

Leaving the road, his aching legs reminded him of just how luxurious his most recent hiking had been, the hill working hard to make every muscle scream as he propelled himself up the steep incline. It hadn't looked like that from the road, but Tyler was now too far along to turn back, stubborn pride forcing him forward. He had to admit to himself that the possibility of sleeping *inside* a building versus amongst the trees was intoxicatingly motivating.

Arriving at the wooden shack, Tyler knelt and watched the building, looking for anything that would indicate it was still in use or that it was being monitored. The shingles on the roof were warped and covered with moss, the walls having faded and cracked from sun exposure over many years. Two windows looked out over the area where the old road would be, but that was all Tyler could see for internal vantage points. Staying low, he approached the side of the building, finding even the flat clearing where the structure sat to be tattered and jagged, the gravel left to the mercy of the weather.

Once at the wall, he went to the back corner and looked around at the area behind the cabin. It was here that he found the entrance. A wooden screen door hung haphazardly from the door frame, while the main door itself was closed. He could see that the door handle had been removed at some point in the past, leaving a dark opening in its place. Tyler was confident that it was no longer in use, and, looking up at the area above the door, he smiled when he saw an old, rusted video camera hanging from a frayed wire. The wire was cut about two feet from the camera itself, a staple being the only thing now keeping the surveillance relic from falling to the ground.

Pushing the door open, Tyler stepped into what appeared to be an abandoned monitoring station. A few of the walls had tables pushed up against them, and sitting on the tables themselves were monitors that hadn't been in production for a few decades. The monitors were coated in a thick layer of dust, and sat on top of square boxes that had a number of buttons and switches on them. Tyler believed that was where the footage would record, but this stuff looked to be older than he was, so he wasn't positive.

There was enough light left in the day for him to make out the rest of the interior. A wood stove sat against one wall, which still had blackened burners on top. There was no sink or washroom, but seeing as how they were out in the wilderness, nature's restroom was only a twenty foot walk away.

It wasn't much of a building anymore, but it would absolutely do the trick for him tonight. He walked to the stove and rapped his knuckles on the burners, not totally sure why, but feeling like it was something his dad would've done in this situation. Turning, he saw a faded map on the wall near the monitors. Moving to it, he grinned when he saw that it was a map of the area surrounding Twin Lake. His grin turned to a full blown smile when he saw a star near a marked roadway, the universal symbol for *you are here.*

The map was oriented so that it was on the wall with North facing up. The land within the valley made a natural circle surrounded by the mountains on all sides. Tyler used his finger and traced from the area where he parked to where he'd crossed the perimeter in the south west corner, and then tried his best to follow along until he arrived at his current location. He found the North West and South West quadrants to be mostly void of anything noteworthy, although far up in the North West quadrant was a small square and a penciled in notation that read '*body dump.*'

He noticed a circle with a small line in the middle and some jagged lines around it, which he estimated to be roughly the place where he'd discovered the beeping speaker. He hoped like hell that someday he'd forget the sight of those animals being destroyed by the steel teeth from below.

Scanning the paper, he found the North East to have a few things marked off. A square with the words '*crash pad*' and a triangle with the word '*medic.*'

The south east section looked to be the major hub of this military property.

A long, thick line made in black ink with the word '*runway,*' was at the farthest right on the map, followed by some squares that Tyler presumed were buildings. Beside the squares were an almost two-inch circle with the notation '*testing grounds.*'

Testing grounds? Tyler had no idea what that meant but he was certain of the dread it filled him with when reading it. Maybe this was where they'd perform live round testing or combat simulations? This was a world very far from his own.

The one bit of knowledge he tried to burn into his head were the small squares peppered throughout a number of the quadrants. While this information was old and most likely outdated, the description of '*cameras*' could only be a benefit. He would do his best to remain away from these areas.

As the sun slipped behind the mountains and darkness descended on the valley, Tyler worked quickly to get together some discarded items to make a fire and offer some warmth to keep the chill off for as long as possible. He'd not seen anything to indicate a fire here would bring unwanted attention, and he had a sense of security with the walls around him. It was a security he'd not felt since he left the house. He couldn't be too confident though.

Believing it to be too obvious, he opened the metal door of the wood stove, cringing at the loud squeal of the hinges. To his surprise, the stove had been cleaned out before the place had been abandoned. Tyler broke the nearest chair and grabbed some faded stacks of paper from a short shelf and had a fire started in no time.

Tyler left the shack briefly once he was confident the fire wouldn't sputter out, needing to relieve his bladder. His water intake had been too low that day, so while he pissed, he made a mental note to drink more the next day, to work harder to prevent dehydration. Standing under the clear sky with a cabin behind him refilled him with the smells and sounds of nature his soul needed. It helped to push away that sense of foreboding, of being watched by something unseen, non-mechanical.

As he turned to walk back, his foot kicked something and a loud *thunk* sounded. Kneeling, he found an old bear trap that he'd accidentally set off.

Jesus, that would have been the end of me, he thought, examining the hunk of metal. It had been set many years ago, the hinges thick with rusted buildup. He traced the metal edging of each tooth as well as the length of corroded chain that was partially buried.

Returning to the cabin, Tyler took one last look at the valley that stretched out as far as his eyes could see. He wished his dad were there with him. He longed to reunite, to find Neil and give the man a hug again.

It took him a moment to realize that he'd been staring at

something to his right and up the side of the valley. He blinked a few times, wondering if he was seeing something or if his eyes were playing tricks on him. His brain worked through the possible explanations, but there was only one that made sense.

He knew exactly what that was.

The flickering of a campfire.

But whose fire was it? *Soldiers? Indigenous people who still inhabited the area? His dad?*

He didn't dare investigate in the darkness, especially after the accidental discovery of that bear trap.

Somebody was out there and they were close.

Luckily, his fire was only producing smoke through the rickety chimney.

For now, he wouldn't be detected, but he knew exactly where he would be going first thing in the morning.

22

THE EARLY MORNING FOG, BOTH OUTSIDE THE SHACK AND inside Tyler's head, kept him from remembering where he was when he rolled over.

The fire he'd made had long since burned out, but the building remained insulated enough to keep some residual heat. This, coupled with having slept under a roof, left him momentarily confused and believing he'd woken up in his room.

Once he attempted to stand and his body reminded him that he'd slept on an abandoned wood floor, it all returned.

The most pressing thing, though, was the remembrance of the glowing orange of the burning fire. *Who'd been out there?* Tyler had attempted a few guesses, but from the odd and horrible things he'd encountered so far he knew it could be anything.

He wanted to get started on the day, but he lingered on the decision to unpin a map and bring it with him. His hesitancy was if he took it and someone came by, they'd notice it was missing. Instead, he took one long last look at it before leaving the cabin. He worked his way back down the steep hill he'd struggled to climb yesterday. Going down was considerably easier, but Tyler still had to be careful. His legs were still feeling mushy from the constant exertion, and one wrong step would be all it took for him to lose his footing and careen head over heels.

Reaching the bottom, he returned to the road and, feeling buoyed by the confidence that this section wasn't being monitored, he set off at a faster pace.

Even surrounded by the trees, Tyler could make out the top of the hill where the flames had been. It gave him an 'x' on his visual map, which for whatever reason, seemed to be what he needed. When he and his dad had gone on hikes, he'd always enjoyed the ones more when they were going *somewhere*, some place that signified they'd made it. He was never sure why; it just gave him a sense of purpose but also security. It was the hikes that had no destination, just a timeline of walking for a week or two before returning, that always left him feeling anxious and unsure. Tyler was fighting this internal battle during his search for Neil. Each day his only 'destination' had been his dad. But his feet felt lighter and his legs were stronger when he had *somewhere* to walk. And this morning, that somewhere wasn't far at all.

The air was cooler at this time of day, the sun not yet over the ridge of the basin. Tyler could see a thin cloud covering already, which had him concerned. If those clouds remained once the sun was up, the air would become muggy and thick, making everything harder. At his current elevation, he was handling the thinner air, but if his lungs had to struggle with humidity as well, he'd need to rest more often.

Bird's singing and a gentle breeze blowing allowed Tyler to focus on the here and now, the joy of being alone in nature. He was a boy born into this environment. This should've felt like a homecoming for his soul, not a tortured journey to find his dad.

Tyler searched for the top of the mountain again, which prevented him from seeing the chunk of metal on the road. His foot hit it and as he began to fall, he wind milled his arms in a frantic attempt to stay standing. This was all in vain, tumbling to the ground with a thud. He rolled onto his side, checking himself over to make sure he wasn't injured. *Just some scrapes.* Getting back to his feet, he examined the area only to find he'd entered a graveyard of discarded vehicles. Beside him was a bent and misshapen steering wheel, half buried on the side of the road. More pieces of metal littered the forest floor, the edges of each section jagged. In some places the material appeared to be melted and deformed.

That could only be possible from extreme heat, Tyler thought, running his finger over the edge. *Could an explosion cause that?*

He hadn't come across anything yet that suggested he was in a blast radius area.

It left Tyler with more questions, but with the mindset of 'moving forward', he left the field of scattered parts, keeping the hillside front and center in his mind.

The feeling of being watched returned, squirming into his head. It was sudden and almost palpable. He came to a dead stop, doing a full circle searching for the culprit. Seeing nothing, he closed his eyes, hoping they'd move and he'd hear them making a sound. Still nothing. Reopening his eyes, he took a deep breath and re-examined his surroundings.

His breath caught in his lungs when he saw it.

The man was half embedded in a thick cedar tree, twenty paces from where Tyler's stood. It looked as though the man had attempted to jump *through* the tree, with his arms stretched before him. *Like Superman*, Tyler thought. The man's face was frozen in a grimace of excruciating pain; eyes wide, lips tight. The section of his chest that was protruding from the tree showed he'd been in full march gear. The butt-end of his rifle was still visible, the rest lost to the tree. His uniform still showed the military insignia.

Tyler wished he could read what the patch said, but there was one problem.

The embedded man was twenty feet off the ground.

How the fuck...?

This one scared and confused Tyler. How did something like this occur?

He found a golf ball sized rock and heaved it towards the man in the tree. The rock sailed true and on target before it arced down and landed with a thud somewhere in the trees. Tyler attempted to hit the soldier a dozen more times before one finally connected.

To Tyler's horror the rock struck the man solidly, knocking his right arm completely off. He jogged to where it landed and poked at it with his boot, unsure of what he was looking at. It had once been skin and bones and veins and blood. Now, upon closer examination, the inside of the appendage had layers and rings. The man had been petrified into wood, the tree claiming it as its own.

"Jesus, fuck," Tyler exclaimed, stepping back in repulsion.

It may have been a trick of his eyes, but he was certain the trees crouched in, the forest darkened, and every living beast in the woods roared and screeched in unison.

Tyler dropped to his knees and covered his ears with his hands. Eyes tightly closed, he focused on the *lub, lub* of his blood pumping. It grounded him, centering his panic and allowing him to exhale.

After several deep breaths, he stood finding the trees tall, the sun shining, and the animals silenced.

He looked one more time at the wooden soldier before continuing onwards to where the flames had been.

Standing at the base of the hill, Tyler looked up to roughly where the flames would have been. The sun had erupted over the valley and with its arrival the temperature had abruptly risen. His sweat was sticky and an annoyance, and Tyler knew he couldn't spend much time out from the tree cover before he'd need to worry about heat exposure.

About a quarter of the way up the hill there was an area not covered in green. No trees or foliage of any kind. It had looked further up from the cabin which he suspected was because of the angle from where he was. There was a crudely made pathway ascending up the rocky hill, which he'd use. He started down the road, looking for the start of the path when he found two things.

The first was what he'd been searching for; the beginning of the path.

The second was the end of the disused road. He could see where the tracks ended and a paved road began and continued off into the woods. A cement barricade sat at the point where the pavement began, designed to prevent any motorized vehicles from driving on the abandoned section. His mind went into overdrive. If he followed this road it would take him to the area marked on the map, he had no doubts about that. Just *what* it would lead him to was still a complete unknown.

As much as the prospects of the paved road excited him, he still needed to find out if the location of the campfire had any clues for him. Someone may still be up there watching him even now. He made his way carefully up the path, finding that a staircase had been hobbled together. At some point, someone had taken the time to scrape out or shovel away some of the hill to create steps. They were uneven and had different lengths and widths, but they'd do.

When he'd made his way above the tops of the trees, he turned and looked over the valley. It offered a stunning view. He took in as much as he could, pushing down the voice in his head telling him to *hurry up, go find dad*. No matter the circumstance, a view like this was one to behold, to take in and appreciate.

He took one last look, ready to turn and keep moving, when Tyler saw what he could only describe as anomalies. Areas of thicker vegetation. Places where the trees either looked artificial or painted. *Masking attempts? Camouflage from above?* Tyler wasn't sure, but he was keen to discover what those areas were hiding. It didn't surprise him at all that the paved road headed off in that direction.

Looking upwards, Tyler saw he was fifty feet from where an area had been cleared of vegetation. From here he could make out odd discrepancies. He prepared himself for what he may discover, but he knew, ultimately, this was the entire reason he'd hiked to this spot.

The last few steps were the hardest he'd ever taken, even more difficult than when he'd discovered the plane wreckage.

He took the final step and his stomach lurched as he saw that the discrepancies weren't just gouges in the mountainside.

They were prison cells.

Caves dug out of the side of the hill to keep people in. *Or things.* That thought popped into his mind and sent a cold shudder down his spine. Tyler was beside himself. The cell doors were fashioned from sticks and rope. A stack of dirty and discarded slop plates sat at the entrance of each opening. He wanted to turn and hurl himself from the path, hoping his brain would shut off somewhere between here and the ground.

Had his father been brought here? Had his mother? Were they killed in these cells?

Tyler went to step into the first cell to inspect it, when a voice to his right scared him so badly he lost his footing and started to topple over the edge.

23

Tyler frantically swung his arms, hoping to grab anything to prevent his fall. Suddenly someone grabbed him, pulling him back from the edge of the steps.

Seeing his savior, he was in disbelief over who stood beside him.

"Officer Carson?"

Tyler had never been more excited to see a police officer than he was now.

"You didn't listen to a damn thing I said, did you?" Carson said.

"You *actually* thought I was going to go for a relaxing hike and not search for my dad?"

The two burst into laughter at the absurdity of the situation.

"My dad's out here too. Somewhere. He's probably long gone, but I've never stopped looking."

This caught Tyler by surprise. He'd never expected that.

"Wasn't your dad a cop?"

"He was. Before I tell you why I'm here, I have something to show you. After, let's hike back down so we can chat. This staircase always freaks me out."

Tyler agreed, following the man to the entrance of the nearest opening.

"Here," Carson said, handing him his flashlight. "I've been in these cages hundreds of times, always looking for clues. Never seen this before until last night when my fire caught the wall just right. It's at the back."

Taking the flashlight, he had to crouch as he entered the cave and made his way to the back. The section of the back wall where Carson had splashed water on was easy to discern. The initial fear he'd felt entering the cave went away upon seeing the wall. He'd been worried that Carson was somehow tricking him into entering only to close the door and trap him. But now, seeing the three names inscribed on the back wall made Tyler trust Carson with all of his heart. The two had more in common than he'd first thought. He ran his fingers over each individual letter, tracing every slash and edge. His mother had been here.

Examining the letters closer, something dawned on him. Judging from how his and his dad's name were carved into the wall, compared to the way his mom's name was slightly larger with more exaggerated scratches, two different people had carved those names.

His dad had been here.

As much as he wanted to remain and run his fingers over this connection to his mom, and more evidence he dad was alive, he turned and went back out to Carson. He returned the flashlight to the cop, thankful to be outside again, an unexpected weight leaving his back when he stood up straight.

"Thank you," he said.

"Welcome," Carson replied.

The two descended in silence. The only sounds were their boots hitting the steps and the occasional rock tumbling around them.

Once back on solid ground, Tyler looked long and hard at the paved road heading deeper into the forest.

"How about we have some coffee and a chat? Then we'll decide what our next move is," Carson said, pulling out some instant coffee mix. Tyler thought back to dumping out the last bit of coffee back in Golden. He wasn't going to offend Carson by declining the drink and in truth, he could probably handle some caffeine.

"So, those were your flames I could see from the shack last night?"

"Shack?"

"I found an abandoned monitoring station," Tyler said, pointing back across the hillside to where the shack was. "It was no longer in use, but provided a roof and four walls, which was a nice change."

"Were there any numbers or markings to indicate just what it might have been called?"

Tyler thought for a minute, not remembering anything like that. Then something did ding his memory.

"There was a map on one of the walls. It had 'MS-145' on the top corner. Does that stand for Monitoring Station 145?"

Carson grabbed his pack, opened a side pocket and retrieved something that Tyler couldn't see. He knelt on the paved road and unfolded it, until it was large enough that Tyler got a good look.

A map.

The officer must have been making it himself, a modern-day voyager, with roughly drawn rivers, roads and buildings. Carson took a pen from his breast pocket, clicked it and added to the map at the approximate spot Tyler had indicated. Tyler joined the man, looking at what had been placed on it so far and tried to see if he could add anything from his memory of the map from the station.

He filled in a few blanks Carson didn't have. Carson was thankful, jotting it down. Looking at what the cop had done so far, Tyler was shocked to see over twenty marked monitoring stations as well as another dozen areas that were clearings.

"Have you seen the animals head to those clearings?" he asked, wondering if Carson had witnessed the slaughter.

"I have."

"So, you know why *I'm* here. You mentioned you were searching for your dad. What happened?"

The two walked from the paved road to sit with their backs against a downed tree.

"My dad suffered a breakdown after your mom's disappearance. He was a lifetime cop. It was a family job, you know? Hell, my grandpa was a cop before him, so it was in our makeup to solve the crime, find the missing. Never stop. All the usual cop talk, you know? Well, your mom is reported missing. He gets a group of volunteers from the town to help with the search. They head off into the woods, wanting to find her. Fuck man... her disappearance... that just ripped our community apart. You were just a baby. Your dad... he was bawling, begging my dad to find her. My dad never told me the details. I found them in his journal after he disappeared."

"What about your mom?"

"She left when I was a kid. Didn't like dad being the cop in town, didn't like the looks, the talk behind her back. She packed up and left, saying I was better off being here with him. Haven't seen her since."

Tyler couldn't believe the similarities between the two of

them, even if their moms had not been in their lives because of different reasons.

"So, one day, I wake up and dad's already got breakfast ready. Sits me at the table and tells me he needs to find the missing lady. I mean, by this time it's been years since your mom vanished. But something is calling him. He left a list of numbers if I needed help and an envelope. He knew he was never coming back. Inside the envelope was his journal and $100,000. Guess he wanted to make sure I'd have money for food, bills, power to keep the lights on."

He stopped, took a drink, and stared into the distance. Tyler was processing as much as he could, but he felt himself growing impatient. He wanted to keep moving, but he didn't want to be disrespectful and make Carson feel like an inconvenience.

"My dad's journal told a sobering story. He'd written it during the search for your mom. They were met by a heavy military presence. They told him the area was private property, punishable by execution. They made him sign a statement saying the woman was presumed dead and the search was off. Then they gave him a check for $100,000. Which he gave to me."

"Did his journal say anything else?"

Carson nodded, finishing off the last of his coffee.

"It described his continued trips into the area in search of her and the mysterious things he found. The clearings of death, the pits of bodies, the screams at night, the beasts from the dark. He remarked often in his writings that either he was losing his mind, or that the land he was visiting was a secret the military wanted to protect but was responsible for creating. He had jotted down a rough section where he believed your mom was, which I've been trying to hike to, but it's been slow going."

This last bit made Tyler perk up.

"Is it in this quadrant?" he asked, pointing to the section of the map that looked to have an airport.

"It is. I did some off-the-books digging. I found that because of where this land sits, technically it is a National Park, so a lot of the records were not available in provincial searches. But the bits and pieces I was able to uncover indicated there is a substantial amount of power and water being sent into an area of land that isn't supposed to exist. When I had one of our computer techs do some hacking for me, he was able to also discover old land purchase records from the 1960's. Seems back then the Canadian Government sold this valley to the Military and the Military turned around and sold it back to themselves. It didn't make sense when I first saw the records, but when I was reading my dad's journal, it started to connect. This is another level altogether."

"So, if I'm understanding what you're saying, we're dealing with something even higher than the Military?"

"I believe so, yes," Carson said, hoisting his pack back on. "Let's get a move on. We've got a few hours of daylight left and I know another shack we can hole up in tonight, then tomorrow we can attempt to get to where I've not made it yet. The base."

"How come you've never made it all the way?"

"I've come close a few times. You'll see one reason for yourself when we get there. Did you notice a section of forest in the distance that looked fake?"

"Like the trees were painted?" Tyler replied.

"Yup. You'll see why soon enough."

Carson examined his watch, then pushed a button.

"I've marked signal spots along the way. You'll see a white dot every 750 meters. At each white dot, we need to stand still for thirty seconds as the camera's swivel. We'll be standing in the blind spot and can continue once my alarm vibrates."

Tyler got his pack situated comfortably and the two started off down the road, keeping to the left-hand side. This had been Carson's recommendation, based on where he said the cameras were located.

They walked at a fast pace, quicker than Tyler would've travelled on his own, but it matched the speed if he'd been hiking with his dad. To once again have a companion in the outdoors was a morale boost. Something Tyler didn't know he wanted, or needed, as much as he did.

For two will create warmer memories than one.

It was a sentiment his dad said so frequently on their trips that they'd even had a sign made and placed over their door at the house. This was what Tyler was experiencing now. With Officer Carson as a partner on this search, Tyler knew any obstacles coming would be far easier to overcome.

"Stop," Carson said. He pointed at a dollar sized white dot on the road. Tyler would never have noticed those if Carson hadn't pointed it out. They moved to the spot and waited while Carson watched the countdown on his watch.

"OK," Carson said, after the thirty seconds were up. They continued, stopping and waiting every 750 meters.

"We're two more stops away from the shack. We'll be able to have a fire. I think what this abandoned station has inside will interest you as well."

They remained silent, the wilderness offering its own soundtrack to this leg of their travels. Tyler identified each of the animals calling out; eagle, moose, elk, and coyote. But it was the animal after the coyote that stopped Tyler and Carson dead in their tracks. The cop looked over, eyes wide.

"I've heard that one a few time," Carson said. "It sounds close."

"I've heard it. I almost saw it. Along the river's edge. If I'd been a split second faster I would've seen it, but all I saw was trees moving from where it went."

"That's a good sign. The fact that *that* animal chose to grace you with its presence and then spoke to you. The Indigenous in the area would say you are blessed."

"I think that call happened for a reason," Tyler said.

From off in the wilderness the animal bellowed again, closer than before.

"Did that sound like a warning?"

Carson looked around, scanning the road and the trees beside them.

They both heard a low rumble at the same time.

"Vehicle!"

Tyler grabbed Carson's arm and pulled him off the road. They both dropped to the ground, pressing themselves as flat as they could, just as two Jeeps careened around the corner and roared past. Tyler went to stand, but Carson pressed his back, indicating he should stay. A third Jeep went by, but this one was different from the previous two. The engine had been modified, the Jeep not making a sound.

"How did you know it was coming?" Tyler asked.

"I felt the vibrations after the other two had gone."

"Thank you. That wouldn't have been good."

"Wonder where they are going in such a rush?" Carson said.

"You think it has anything to do with our unexpected warning system?"

Carson didn't reply, but the look of concern etched on his face was answer enough.

"OK, let's get going. Eyes and ears on full alert," Carson said, leading the way.

They continued to the next white dot and paused, then carried on to the last white dot. Once the thirty seconds were up, Carson motioned for Tyler to follow and they left the paved road. Tyler found they were on an old footpath. The space between the trees and underbrush was parted perfectly for them.

Carson walked with the confidence of someone who's traversed the path numerous times. Tyler suspected he'd be able to make this walk in the dark or with his eyes closed. Another two hundred meters and Carson motioned for them to stop. Looking past the officer, a clearing opened up and he was immediately filled with panic. He knew the monitoring station was near, but did they need to find a way across a killing clearing?

"The shack is just across that clearing. Don't worry, this isn't like the clearing you saw before. I'm always cautious though just in case something's changed since the last time I was here," Carson whispered.

Carson crouched low and approached the clearing's edge. Once there, he picked up a rock and tossed it into the middle. It landed with a dull thud. They held their breath, waiting for some sort of reaction; an alarm, a siren or a set of metal blades exploding from the ground.

When nothing happened for what felt like an eternity, Carson stood and removed something from a pocket on the side of his pants. He brought the whistle to his lips and gave it two quick blasts. Again they waited, and once again nothing happened.

"We're good. No motion detection, no sound detection, and no ground force detection. We'll skirt the perimeter. The shack is directly across from us."

Carson started to his left, keeping just inside the trees. Tyler followed, looking as hard as he could to find the structure, but was unable to even make out the shape of a building. It took them half an hour to make their way around the edge. When they finally arrived at the opposite side, Carson stepped deeper into the trees putting the clearing behind them.

A half dozen paces followed before Carson stepped aside and pointed. Tyler stood staring at nothing but trees.

"Am I supposed to be looking at the world's greatest camouflaged structure?"

Carson smirked and pointed up. Tyler followed the cop's finger and smiled.

Twenty feet up in the trees a monitoring station had been built.

Carson approached and moved aside some strategically placed branches and downfall, before pulling free an older rope ladder.

"Take your time, the ladder likes to swing," he said as he began climbing. He hadn't been lying. The ladder wanted to twist and sway as Carson ascended.

Tyler took one last look around, before grabbing hold and following.

24

———

It was a struggle just to make it from one rung to the next, but thankfully it wasn't that high of a climb.

Halfway up, Tyler noticed the trunk of the tree. Or rather, he noticed the thick slash marks that crisscrossed the bark. Something immense had attacked this tree in the past. Tyler wondered if whatever left the marks had been chasing someone up the ladder or trying to get into the station.

Carson stopped at the top of the ladder and unlatched several different closing mechanisms before forcefully pushing the wooden section above him. The entrance latch swung up and into the station, hitting the floor with a bang that was louder than Tyler wished. Carson hoisted himself up, before turning and offering a hand. Tyler accepted and climbed into the station, but not before feeling that moment of fear when his feet remained exposed below. It was a similar feeling to when something would graze your legs while swimming. A *'what the fuck was that'* dread.

The interior of the station was surprising, considering what it looked like from the ground. It wasn't much different than the other abandoned monitoring building he'd spent the night in. Four walls, tables along three of them. The main difference here was no fireplace and no traditional door. The fourth wall, the one that would have hosted the door, had been instead utilized as an impressive bulletin board.

"This is what I thought would get your attention," Carson said, sealing the latch and approaching the board. Tyler joined him, staring at what was displayed on the wall.

Photo after photo of *things* were tacked to the board. Creatures from the darkest recesses of Tyler's nightmares.

Most had been taken from the windows up here, the higher vantage point evident by the angle of the picture, while some had been taken at the base of the tree, the rope ladder in the background. Others had been taken nearby, the subjects in the photos near a Jeep on a paved road.

He took his time examining each one, before returning to the beginning and started again. After three trips through the dozens and dozens of photos, Tyler turned to Carson.

"Are these real?"

"Absolutely," Carson replied.

Tyler couldn't believe his eyes. While most of the photos were blurry, which was probably due to the subject moving when it was taken, he was still able to make out details that unnerved him.

In one photo taken from the monitoring station, an immense bear was walking below. It must have been easily ten feet at the shoulders. In another, three large wolves sat, eagerly looking up at the photographer. While this in itself wasn't anything out of the ordinary considering their location, what made the photo surreal was that the wolves were at least triple the size of normal wolves. Photo after photo showed an animal that appeared to be morphed, made significantly bigger than the regular version. It was the middle section of the bulletin board that the photos really frightened him.

He looked at a two-headed bull, standing in the clearing. Even from a distance the bull was impressive, but with nothing to show scale, Tyler could only guess at its height. Instead of two horns on each head, the animal had four on each, making it look as though it had antlers.

The last batch of photos were the hardest to look at. In one, a man sat beside an animal that was strewn across a trailer behind a Jeep. The animal was too dark to determine the species, but Tyler almost puked when he realized the beast possessed human arms. No fur, no dark hair, but honest to God human arms. A moose was in the next photo with a normal front half. Looking closely, Tyler could see that its back end appeared to be wood, much like the soldier he'd come across previously. Another photo featured a lynx dragging itself along the ground, its hind end consisting of tentacles trailing behind it. The round suckers were clearer in the photo, even with such poor focusing. The next picture was of a soldier sitting in the driver's seat of a Jeep. He had one hand on the wheel while the other was wrapped around the shoulders of his passenger. The passenger had the head of a bear. While the photo only showed the passenger from waist up, the torso and chest was that of a nude female, bare breasts visible through the windshield.

"Look here," Carson said, pointing at the last photo.

Tyler had to crouch down to get a better view, but even after all of the other photos he'd seen this one was tough to look at.

"That can't be? Can it? My *guide*," he said, reaching a hand out and touching the photo as if to confirm it was real.

The photo had been taken from the middle of a clearing. A flock of birds was flying away from a massive, horned creature that stood in the middle and was looking towards the photographer. It must have been twenty feet tall, with horns that sprouted out to the sides ten feet from its head in either direction. The creature looked to be smiling at the person behind the camera, head tilted down with its mouth open in a sly grin. Tyler felt equally calm and afraid looking at what had been bellowing to him over the last few days. He could see this scene play out as though he'd been there. Standing twenty feet behind the photographer, the rain falling as the mighty beast walked into view and stopped to look over at them. The birds took flight as the man raised his camera and snapped the photo. He could almost feel the drops of rain on his face.

It actually reminded him of an old grainy YouTube video that everyone insisted was a hoax, but Tyler secretly hoped was real. It showed a Mastodon crossing a river somewhere in the wilderness, and he'd probably watched the clip a thousand times, if not more.

"I can't believe it."

Tyler was stunned.

"The first time I saw these photos, I wanted to take them with me. I wasn't sure why or what I'd do with them, maybe scan them and put them online? But then I realized that would put a direct target on me. I'm sure someone somewhere is aware of my intrusions here, keeping tabs on me. But taking the photos would be too much. So, I left them. But I never stop thinking about them, about what's shown in them. It's just... wow."

Tyler nodded. He understood what Carson meant. His first thought was to take a few and hold them close. To look at them over and over. They were magical, but also the type of thing that would keep you awake at night, knowing that these beasts existed.

"I know I'm going to be looking at these photos a lot before it's too dark, but what else is in the station?"

Carson gave Tyler a brief tour, showing him the old monitors and the CB radio set up, which he said still let out static and, once in a while, a garbled word or two.

"Scared the shit out of me the first time I was here. Suddenly a word was spoken and I thought I'd been discovered. Once I figured out it was from this, I spent the next few hours surfing the channels, trying to pick up anything else. It was probably interference from a plane or something overhead. I turned the sound completely off though. Didn't want another fright."

This station also had a map on one wall. The difference here was colored pushpins had been poked in dozens of spots.

"Any idea on what they reference?" Tyler asked.

"No clue. The closest I can gather is some are clearings, some are bunkers, and some are monitoring stations. There's no legend with this map, but I've compared it to my own and that's what I suspect."

Tyler moved to the window and looked at the clearing. From here his view was mostly blocked, but a few small openings let him see some of the bare forest floor they'd walked around.

"Just what the hell is going on here, Carson?"

"I don't know. I really don't. The government is hiding something, and the military is definitely doing research they don't want known, but for why and for what? I'm in the dark just as much as you are."

Carson pulled something from underneath a table. Setting it down, Tyler marveled at the cobbled-together fire hold.

"Every time I came I brought parts with me and glued it

together. It allows me to have a fire and not burn the place down," Carson said with a shrug, seeing Tyler's grin.

The two got a fire started using wood that Carson had gathered previously and hidden in a storage box.

As another day grew closer to an end, Tyler went back to the photos and sat cross-legged. It was all so much to take in, to let his mind understand that all of these photos were *real*.

"I'll let you have some time to look at the photos. I'm just going to sit over here and meditate, if that's all the same to you. I've spent too many hours already memorizing those," Carson said, taking a seat near the fire.

Tyler didn't mind. A little quiet was always a welcome way to end a day in the woods. Silent reflection. Only this time, Tyler was going to spend his time taking in the insanity tacked to the wall.

It didn't matter where he let his eyes fall, madness was what he found. A three-legged animal with wide, membranous wings. Its head was shaped like a spear and Tyler couldn't find anything that resembled eyes. He saw a snake-headed man, whose skin was covered in scales and their hands had no fingers, just layers formed into rattles. On and on it went, horror after horror. But Tyler found himself continually drawn to the blurry photo of the massive creature in the clearing. That beast had guided him, helped him when he needed it. Was it the same? Probably not. But, then, Tyler found it even more improbable that there were two of the animals roaming this land. He shook his head in disbelief. It was hard to accept.

As the sun set and the flames lowered, the light dimmed enough that he couldn't look any longer. He took a spot on the other side of the flame hold and settled on the floor, using his pack as a pillow. Carson was already asleep. Tyler closed his eyes, not sure what the next day would bring. He wondered how close they were to his dad.

Before he drifted off, he thought once more of the antlers that travelled so very far away from that creature's head.

The surge of electricity ripped through Neil as he strained against the strapping that bound him to the bed. He thrashed and wailed, lips cracked and bleeding. The shadowed figure beside his bed snapped their fingers and the attendant in the darkened corner twisted the dial. A hum sounded and the machine crackled as another course buried its way into Neil's body.

He screamed like the mad man he was now, begging to be released. The thick canvas wraps on his wrists dug in and cut through his skin. Neil almost would have preferred metal cuffs, even if they melted into his arms.

"Once more?" the figure asked, wondering if the patient had experienced enough.

"Yes, but double it up, the legs are still not responding."

Neil tried to look at the person in the lab coat beside him, but all he heard was the snap of their fingers, the machine powering up, and the feeling that his eyeballs had burst from his skull.

25

Sometime in the middle of the night, a massive predator let out a roar that shook the station. Tyler and Carson sat bolt upright. The moon was bright enough to illuminate some of the forest around them, but neither spotted movement.

"Just what in the fuck was that?" Tyler asked.

"No idea," Carson replied, "but I bet it's over there in one of those photos."

Another roar ripped through the darkness.

It had such an intensity and violence to it that Tyler felt his bones rattle. Whatever it was, it was both near and far. Tyler couldn't explain that sensation. It just was. Most likely it was the forest playing tricks on how the sound travelled. That explanation didn't make him feel any better.

He was about to ask Carson a question when he noticed he was motioning for him to not speak.

For a brief moment the night was dead silent.

Then Tyler heard it.

A beeping.

"Is that from the clearing here?"

"I think so," Carson replied. "Jesus. Was this done while we were sleeping? Surely we would've heard them?"

Rustling from below the station got their attention, and, looking down from their perch, they watched as animal after animal walked past them in a hypnotic parade and headed straight for the clearing.

A braying noise followed, accompanied by the metallic unsheathing and deafening explosion as an animal was eviscerated 100 meters from them. Even in the dead of night, both men could picture the creature moving in a daze towards the sound, then the explosion of the metal blades appearing from the earth and the horrible painting that would appear for a moment in the night sky as the animals insides became outsides before transforming into a fluid mixture and splattering to the ground.

Carson started another fire, knowing neither of them would be able to fall back asleep. Once it was going, he closed the window blinds to limit the glow from the outside.

The two sat around the small heat source for the next few hours, trying like hell to block out the sounds.

26

––––––––––

Morning brought puffy eyes and aching backs.

The two hadn't been able to get any sleep, instead sitting in silence as the flames died out and the forest animals continued to die. At one point, Carson had returned to the window, peeking through a small slit he'd made to try and see what was happening. He returned with wide eyes and a tenseness to his face that suggested he'd seen *something*, but for the preservation of them remaining hidden, he'd kept quiet. Tyler decided to wait and ask in the morning.

Just before dawn, something of significant size bashed into the main tree that the station was moored on. The rope ladder clanked as it flew around uncontrolled, and the entire station shuddered and threatened to topple from its perch. Shortly after, the creature let out a roar before the familiar sound of the blades destroying the animal followed. Soon after, a horn blared and an air-raid siren blasted for thirty seconds. Following that, the forest returned to stark stillness.

They waited until the sun was up and the early dew had disappeared before feeling confident enough to descend.

Carson went first. He unlatched the hatch and examined the rope ladder. Luckily it was still intact, allowing him to climb down. Tyler followed, closing the station entrance after he was through and making sure to secure it. He found a two-foot section of bark that had been ripped off, presumably where the beast had made contact. Seeing the damage it had inflicted, he was surprised the ladder was in ok shape, but maybe the creature hadn't actually hit it dead on.

Walking back through the trees to the clearing, Tyler followed Carson closely. Today, the air felt thicker, the forest tighter, and they both repeatedly looked to see if they were being watched.

At the edge of the clearing, Tyler surveyed the carnage left behind. He'd imagined what the clearing must look like the first time he'd come across a killing field, but to actually stand there and see it was tough. It was an image he'd never forget.

The entirety of the open area was covered in various chunks of animal remains. From here, the two men could see various tusks, snouts, paws and even a few fully intact heads, but for the most part it was a lake of pink-red fluid and gore. The smell that wafted over them was that of innards and shit, enough to make Tyler gag and retch. He turned and spat, deciding that it was disrespectful to spit on the remains of the deceased.

"I've never seen this," Carson said.

"It's something I'll never forget," Tyler replied.

"Let's go," Carson said.

They retraced their steps around the outside edge of the clearing, staying just within the tree line. Once back at the paved road, they looked to see if anything else had changed overnight. Satisfied as best they could be that things were the same, Carson motioned for them to carry on.

Tyler finally worked up the nerve to ask Carson just what he'd seen the night before that had scared him so much.

"I still don't know if I believe it. But... what I think I saw was a man and a woman, attached. Like, they were Siamese twins. Only they had too many arms and both of them... both of them had branches growing out of them. All over. It was as though one of those photos came to life right before me. I watched them until they disappeared into the trees. They were walking towards the clearing."

Tyler realized Carson was on the edge of tears. The *human* aspect was getting to him. How much of that was thinking about his own father? Much like Tyler was struggling with just what had happened to his own parents, Carson was dealing with it as well.

"What is this place?" Tyler finally asked.

"A nightmare. A fucking nightmare."

From a distance, a roar punctuated Carson's statement, causing them both to flinch. They would've normally laughed under different circumstances at the timing of the roar. Instead they walked, making their way to what Tyler still thought of as the 'fake forest.'

Just what had that anomaly been? Carson wasn't giving him anything. Not that Tyler had asked. While they didn't know each other that well, they now had that companionship through shared hardship. Similar to how airplane crash survivors or mass shooting survivors grow and develop friendships. But, Tyler knew when Carson said something, it wasn't worth pushing him on it.

"You think our parents are still alive?"

Carson made a pained noise, as though Tyler had been reading his mind.

"If they've been turned into some science experiment, I hope not."

Another roar sounded.

They looked at each other.

While they didn't have any way of knowing if it was the same creature that had made the noise, it was obvious to both that the roar was significantly closer than the last one.

"Double time," Carson said, which prompted them both to start jogging.

"How far?"

"Not far. Two, maybe three minutes tops," Carson said, scanning the forest to his left with interest.

"You hear that?" Carson said, stopping.

Tyler pulled up and focused.

It took a second but then it grew in volume.

"Is that a helicopter?"

The distinct thrum of a helicopter continued to grow louder and closer. They hustled off the road and hunkered down under a dense tree, its branches having grown close to the ground.

"Something's coming," Tyler said, the ground vibrating under him.

Only fifty meters in front of them, a bear with the horns of a bull burst forth from the trees. The animal was near thirty feet tall, its arrival causing a dozen trees around it to explode or crack and topple. Above it, the helicopter appeared, hovering in place as a soldier leaned out and aimed a rifle at it. The bear turned its immense head towards the chopper and swatted, its massive paw barely missing the landing skids. The helicopter jerked up, putting more distance between it and the colossus. The bear sunk low to the ground, before propelling up, jumping with an impressive display of power, the ground rippling beneath its feet. The beast came up just short of the helicopter again, but the evasive maneuver caused the soldier to topple out and fall from the interior. They never made it to the ground as the bear-bull snapped them up in its massive jaws. Tyler could hear the crunch of bones as the brute chewed. Then the animal turned and rushed further into the woods, away from a stunned Tyler and Carson.

Once they could no longer hear the helicopter, they climbed out from their hiding spot. Standing in silence, neither man moved. Both stared at the prints left behind by the creature.

"I don't believe my mind will ever fully accept what just happened," Tyler said.

"It feels odd to say this, but the coast is clear," Carson replied, causing both to smile.

Carson had been right about how far away they were. After a few minutes' walk they rounded a corner and Tyler couldn't believe what awaited them.

"May I present to you the fake forest," Carson said.

Before them was a fifty-foot-tall concrete wall. It had been completely painted green to try and blend in. Looking across the wall, Tyler could see where it had begun to sprout moss and even roots, the forest slowly beginning to claim it.

"That is massive. Why the hell is something like this out here?" Tyler asked.

"Complete cliché, but I think it's to keep things in *and* out."

"Have you found a way over?"

"Not over, but I've found a way through. The entrance is over there," Carson said, pointing off to their right. "About five hundred meters that way is a section that has cracked and split. I imagine it's from the weather systems that come through here and the ground shifting below. But there's a way through. I've never had the guts to walk all the way to the other side."

Tyler understood.

He couldn't imagine walking further by himself, either.

Not anymore.

27

———

"Can I ask you something?"

"Sure," Carson replied.

The two had left the paved road and were nearing the hidden entrance to the wall.

"The road is paved, right? Well, where does it go? We've seen vehicles drive in that direction. Does the wall open? Does it raise up and the road goes under? It makes no sense."

Carson smiled, looking at Tyler with a tiredness that came from deep in his soul.

"None of this makes sense. The first time I made it this far I stood in disbelief. This wall. This fucking wall in the middle of this godforsaken basin, painted green and growing shit all over it. I was angry. It didn't add up. How did vehicles come from here? If the wall opened surely it would take time to open and close, yet I've never even heard mechanical workings or felt an earthquake sized rumble that would have to happen. Which led me to my current hypothesis. The key is on the other side. I think we'll gain an understanding and frankly, I'm ready to find out."

They ducked under some dead fall and then Carson pointed ahead to a darkened space in the green surface. The site of the entrance gave Tyler pause. He didn't want to go in. Everything inside screamed at him to turn around, find another way, but he knew there wasn't another option.

"And you've not been through?"

"Not all the way. I tried once. I made it about half way when I saw movement at the far end. *Something* was out there," Carson said.

A rumble off in the distance shocked them forward, Carson first with Tyler on his heels. The crack that ran through the wall was large enough that they could stand up inside, but they were immediately enveloped in darkness. The exit ahead was the light guiding them to the far side.

"What *was* that?" Tyler asked, finding he felt the need to whisper.

"I don't know. Maybe a rockslide? It didn't sound like thunder."

Now within the wall, Tyler sensed the enormity of the structure above them. Coupled with the darkness, it became incredibly claustrophobic. In all the years of hiking with his dad, the one thing he steadfastly refused to try was anything related to caving. The thought of tossing on a helmet and some climbing gear to go underground and force his way through tight spaces brought on cold sweats. He was getting that sensation, feeling his heart beating faster, his breathing changing.

Focus on the light ahead. Breathe. Carson's here. You're not trapped.

He told himself that over and over as they walked. The space was bare, with no tripping obstacles or random rocks or chunks of cement in the way. Carson said that he'd scoured the ground each time he'd entered the opening but had always found the short path through clear.

Tyler breathed easy once they arrived at the other side.

"Let's make sure it's safe to leave," Carson said, creeping to the edge before looking both ways. Once he saw that nothing was lurking, they stepped out and surveyed their surroundings.

"Huh. More woods."

Tyler almost laughed at Carson's sarcastic remark, but it was true. They'd left the confines of the wall and found themselves standing in more forest on the other side. The wall on this side was also green and had a significant amount of moss and weeds growing all over it. More than the other side. He didn't know why that thought had any importance to it, but it hung there like a fly caught in a spider web.

This side of the mysterious wall was eerily quiet.

Tyler walked towards the road, wondering what they'd find in this enclosed section of the valley. Carson hung back, examining the cement wall near the crack.

He jogged and caught up to Tyler, grabbing his shoulder and pulling him to a stop.

"You hear that?"

Tyler had now learned to hate that question. In this place it meant running or death.

He listened. He focused, held his breath, but didn't hear anything. He shook his head.

"Listen again," Carson said once more. "There, the hum. Electricity? I haven't heard that at all in this valley before. Not even at the perimeter."

Now that Carson had mentioned it, Tyler *did* hear the hum. But where was it coming from?

"I heard this before from a small shed I came across

built into the hill. It wasn't long after I entered the valley, actually," Tyler said.

Continuing on, Tyler saw a thinning of the trees ahead where the road travelled through them. This was it, they'd find out how vehicles drove under or through an opening in the wall.

"Carson? You seeing this?"

They stopped at the edge of the road in disbelief. The wall was the same as the other side. No sign of an entrance, an opening, or a way to go through. Just an extremely tall slab of concrete that was covered in green.

"I don't understand. There *has* to be a way to go through." Carson said in frustration. Tyler suspected Carson had a hypothesis and this wasn't what he'd expected.

"I don't know what to say man, I really don't. Let's chalk it up to the oddness of our surroundings and keep moving forward?"

Carson nodded but Tyler saw how his shoulders slumped ever so slightly, his head dipping to lower his eyes.

"We'll need to be extra vigilant now. We have no idea what's ahead. Cameras, guard stations, drones. Who knows? But if we keep to the shadows and edges, and move as one, we'll limit the likelihood of detection."

Tyler knew Carson had analyzed and agonized over this exact moment for many hours. Should he get to the other side of the wall and move deeper into the area, what his next moves would be. Now, they were both standing at the precipice of the unknown.

"After you," Tyler said, not wanting to lead. Carson didn't object. Tyler believed it was because of his occupation. The wall created a barrier behind them, which made this section of road stiflingly hot. Tyler didn't believe he'd sweated this much since he started this journey, which had transformed into a mission more than anything. Less a rescue and more of a recovery, as much as he didn't want to admit that out loud.

"The humming's getting louder," Carson said.

It dawned on Tyler that the louder the humming was becoming, the hotter it was getting.

"Something's not right here. The sun's not even above us and it's gotta be close to 40 degrees out. The humming's the source," Tyler said, stopping and wiping his head with his forearm.

"You're right. Look how red your face is. Jesus, am I that red?"

"Yup. Are we being microwaved?"

Tyler said it half-jokingly, but once the words were out of his mouth, they both realized the high probability that this was what *was* happening.

"We need to move," Carson said, breaking into a jog.

Tyler tried to keep up with the man, but found his legs weren't allowing him to speed up. Carson was moving farther and farther ahead, which stoked Tyler's fear of what was happening to him.

"Carson, wait up! *Please*?" He was begging, but he didn't care.

The air was thick enough that Tyler could see it undulating in waves. His vision blurred and the ground shifted like he was walking on soup. His pack felt like it was a thousand pounds on his back, pushing him closer and closer to the liquid concrete he was now practically swimming in. He closed his eyes, the heat too hot, every opening in his head bubbling and frying.

Then hands were on him and he was grabbed hard and

pulled by the straps of his backpack. He lost contact with the ground for a moment before he slammed into it hard and rolled on the rough cement.

Cool air and a light breeze washed over him.

He hesitantly opened his eyes to find Carson standing above him.

"Almost lost you," he said, still panting hard.

"It was like the cement had turned to liquid and I was sinking into it," Tyler said.

"You were. I made it to the end of the humming, and the air changed. I'm sorry, I thought you were right behind me. When I looked back and saw you, you were knee deep in the road and you looked drunk. I got as close as I could before the cement started to shift under my feet and I just grabbed you and pulled as hard as I could."

"Well, thank you."

Carson gave him a *no worries* wave, taking a drink and looking around.

"So, what's the point of this area exactly? Is it a fail-safe? Preventing something from getting to the wall?"

Tyler thought about it but nothing made sense anymore. This valley was wearing his rational mind down to the point of not believing anything he saw, but also accepting that anything was possible.

"You think that's how you get through the wall? To the other side?"

Carson took some time to think about what Tyler suggested, looking back at the hazy section of air between them and the wall.

"I... just don't know, Tyler. Maybe? Maybe it's a perimeter alarm? Fuck, I'm as lost as you are."

That was the first time Tyler saw sheer exhaustion on

the cop's face, but also the first inkling of wanting to give up. Defeated. Looking up at the man, Tyler could see the weight of hopelessness sitting on his back. His shoulders sagged, his chin dropped. Tyler was certain that tears were forming at the edges of his eyes.

"Look, Carson. I just wanted to say thank you for helping me."

"This gonna be a pep talk?"

"Probably. We're both further than you've ever been. We're doing this together. My mom and dad may still be out here somewhere. Your dad. I know this place keeps throwing stuff our way that doesn't make any sense, but we need to keep going. For them. They wouldn't give up on us if our places were switched, and I damn well ain't giving up on them."

He held out his hand, which Carson took and helped Tyler to his feet.

"You're right. Thanks. Gut-check time. We're close. I know we are. Together we got this, right?"

They shook hands and turned, only to find a creature from their worst nightmares standing ten feet away.

"Jesus, what in the fuck is that?"

Carson said it so low that Tyler only heard the first word and the *fuck*, but he filled in the rest.

At one point the animal had begun life as a reptile. Four legs, tail, scales, two beady eyes, darting tongue. Now, they stared at a behemoth of saliva and fangs. Its legs were as thick as tree trunks, tail as long as a bus. When its tongue flitted in and out, the scraping noise it made along its gums caused Tyler's testicles to retract. It filled up the roadway, a construction vehicle made of flesh and bone, ready to rip and thrash.

"We're dead," Tyler whispered. The creature shuffled forward slightly, closing the distance to a point where Tyler suspected it could touch them with its tongue.

Both men instinctively stepped backwards, the humming reminding them that they could go no further. They were out of room.

The lizard-beast slinked sideways; first right then left. It was sizing them up, Tyler knew, deciding which one to eat first and which one to chase after. Its tail thwacked against the trees along the road, strumming them like they were merely guitar strings. The leaking saliva intensified, some strands long enough to reach the surface of the road, growing longer and thinner as the creature moved.

Tyler watched its nostrils flare and the eyes blink, the clear sheath for when it was underwater sliding back and forth over the eyeballs.

"I have an idea," Carson said, tentatively reaching for the pocket on his cargo pants. He popped open the flap and rustled something from inside. When he pulled a small bag out from within, the creature's head snapped to him, nostrils flaring.

"Beef jerky," he said, unable to suppress his smile. "I always keep a slab for emergencies." He held his hand up, shaking the meat around. The creature followed it intently.

"Here you go boy, yeah? You want this?" Carson reared back and let the chunk of jerky go flying as though he was attempting to throw a runner out at home plate. The creature moved with unbelievable speed and its tongue grabbed the hunk of salted beef before it had even travelled twenty feet.

"Fuck," they both said in unison.

It turned its attention back to them.

"You got any more?" Tyler asked. "Please say yes."

"Nope."

It moved a foot closer. Its tongue darted out and licked Carson's arm, then snaked out again, licking Tyler's face. Neither of them dared move, let alone breathe. An almost imperceptible croaking sound was coming from deep inside its gullet, its tongue clicking against the bottom of its mouth.

It was ready to devour them.

Tyler saw the creature's mouth open in slow-motion, watched with a horrified understanding that Carson was going to be crushed in its jaws and that he needed to run, and needed to run *now*. But before the creature could lunge and begin to crush them both, a familiar and much welcomed bellow shook the area.

The effect was instantaneous. The lizard shuddered and slunk back, tucking its legs in close to its body. To their amazement, it slithered back into the trees like the world's largest snake. When the final length of tail disappeared into the woods, both men exhaled.

"Wow. Wow," Carson said, walking in a circle with his hands on his head, looking as though he'd just finished running a marathon.

"I think that is the closest I've ever come to being consumed by a dinosaur," Tyler said.

The two burst out laughing. It felt good to let the tension out, but their laughter didn't last long as another bellow sounded.

"Our mystery guide wants us to get going," Tyler said. They left the electric humming behind them, on edge as they walked past where the lizard-beast had disappeared into the woods.

Silence rejoined them as they continued down the road. No signs of cameras or monitoring stations. Tyler sensed this area was considered 'no man's land.' Where, whoever was in charge, left it to its own devices and passed through it sparingly, only when necessary.

With only the sounds of their boots on the cement, they walked for another hour before they rounded a corner to see rapid motion ahead. It took a moment for them to comprehend that they'd startled a herd of elk and, as the majestic animals scattered and took off into the trees, they continued on. Tyler couldn't believe the relief he felt over seeing regular animals.

"We should stop and rest soon, find a scouting spot. Have some food," Carson said. Tyler agreed. The surroundings were fairly flat, but there were some rolling mounds off to the right.

"That's probably the easiest spot," he said, pointing to one particular mound that was mostly treeless.

"That'll work. Good eyes."

They walked until they were parallel with the mound then left the road and pushed through the trees. The forest wasn't as dense here, the ground almost completely bare of any broken branches or small growth, as it had been on the other side of the wall, which made for easier passage. Carson led the way, as was their routine now. Strangely, Tyler found this was the first time since they'd joined up that being behind the man felt creepy, and he kept looking back to see if something was preparing to attack. He recognized this was because of the way the lizard-thing had ambushed them, the electric hum and the beast's ability to slither like a snake enough to mask its approach. But that didn't change the here-and-now.

The further from the road they were, the nearer Tyler was to a full-on freak out. He actively slowed his breathing, focused on his footsteps and kept his eyes locked on Carson's back.

I'm not alone, he kept repeating in his head.

"Probably best we don't walk out into a clearing here," Carson joked, as they arrived at the edge of the trees. Tyler had been so focused on not losing it that he'd not even noticed they'd walked up the incline to the top of the mound. Carson wasn't aware of Tyler's mental state at the moment, which had him look at Tyler when he didn't even so much as offer a forced chuckle at the attempt at humor.

"You ok?"

"Yeah, just... that beast sneaking up on us really has me freaked."

"Ah, shit. Yeah man. Sorry, I was just trying to lighten the mood."

"All good."

"You fine if I climb up this tree and check out the surroundings?"

Tyler held Carson's pack as the man pulled himself up. The branches were spaced as though the tree had been built with the singular purpose of being used to climb.

"Holy fuck, Tyler. I'm coming down. You *need* to see this. You'll never believe this, and that's saying something."

Tyler didn't even attempt to try and guess what he'd seen as Carson climbed down. He handed both packs to him and made his way up. When he turned and spotted what Carson had been excited about, he smiled.

A complex.

A perimeter fence surrounded something that resembled a prison. Lookout towers were at each corner and even from this distance, activity was visible. Soldiers walked, Jeeps drove, and the gate at the front entrance opened and closed as vehicles came and went. As Tyler started to climb down, he heard a noise and, looking in the sounds direction, he watched a small plane take off and climb high into the sky.

Once he climbed down and stood by Carson, he knew they were thinking the same thing.

Our parents are in there.

But how were they going to get inside?

28

A FAMILIARITY GREETED TYLER AS THEY LEFT THE MOUND AND started towards the complex. Silence. They walked and the trees were still and the animals didn't utter a single noise. If he'd been keeping notes or paying attention since he crossed that perimeter days ago, *although it felt like a year already*, he would've determined that this happened before *and* after any sort of significant event.

He tried to put those incidents in order and couldn't.

Was it mental exhaustion? The toll the journey thus far had taken on him physically? Or a form of early-onset PTSD that was blocking stuff from his mind?

One thing that he never forgot was the ache in his heart when he saw Carson beside him or ahead of him, instead of his dad. Was Neil still alive? Would he get any closure about his mom? Was Carson's dad alive? These questions were filled with hideous dread over what the possible answers were. Now, so close to the complex, did Tyler truly want to find out?

"Are they alive?"

Carson heard Tyler but continued to look forward. Tyler

could see the muscles in his jaw clench and unclench. He mulled it over for another minute, before he found a slab of rock to sit on and took a drink. Once he was done, he looked at Tyler.

"I honestly don't know. And that just crushes me."

For the second time, Tyler was looking at a defeated man.

"No pep talk," Carson said, seeing Tyler's expression.

Tyler held his hands up, palms forward. He stepped back, lowering them and grabbing his drink.

"Look, I'm sorry. It's not the answer either of us wants to hear, but in my line of work I'm trained to understand the worst-case scenario is usually the most probable scenario. My dad has been gone for a while. The likelihood of him still being alive, slim to none. But I'm his son? You know? Fuck sakes. I should be angry at him for abandoning me. But I'm not. I understand why he did it. To find out what happened to your mom, which I think lessens the sting of him just up and leaving. So, he left to find her and now I need to find him. Connectivity. Same purpose, different person. So, really, I'm sorry for being deflated and being negative, but I need to keep a sense of reality to what's happening right now, because nothing makes sense anymore."

Tyler understood. While his mom hadn't left him and his dad hadn't abandoned him, he found himself in the exact same situation as Carson. Alone and searching, looking for answers.

"Carson, I get it. I'm not going to try and give you another pep talk. What I am going to say is this – I need you. I can't do this on my own. But if you are suggesting that you're at the point of giving up and turning back, especially now that we see just *what* exactly we've gotten ourselves into, I get it. I'll go forward and you can head back. No hard feelings. But I need you. I don't know if that means anything at all, but I need you."

Tyler took another sip of water then retrieved a handful of trail mix he still had in his pack. He couldn't bring himself to look directly at Carson, feeling the weight of his words hang in the air between them. Had he been too harsh? Tossing the snack in his mouth, he thought about how he'd be able to continue on alone. Just how difficult it would be to infiltrate this secret military complex. Or, and he hoped this was the case, Carson would keep going.

"I ain't heading back. I don't give up. Every time I've been out here *alone*, I get to a point where something has forced me back. Work commitments, strange beasts, or an increase in soldiers patrolling. Something. This is the farthest I've ever made it and I know we're close to discovering just what the hell is going on in this strange place. So, no. We're in this to the very end, whatever that may be."

The weight of uncertainty lifted off Tyler's shoulders. He hadn't realized just how rigid he'd been standing, waiting for his response.

"I think time moves differently here. It appears we only have an hour or so before the sun's going to set. We should find a place to make camp and then rest up for what will most definitely be an extreme day tomorrow."

29

THEY FOUND A DUG-OUT AREA ON THE SIDE OF A HILL IN THE trees that would work.

The ground had been scooped out by a machine at some point, the visible bucket marks and large equipment tracks giving them more questions to ponder. What were they trying to build here?

They cut some boughs from a nearby tree, making a structure to shelter them from the cold of the night. Carson stated they were too close to the complex to risk a fire, so they did what they could to block the wind and the potential of any unexpected rain. The weather in the mountain bowl seemed to change on a whim. They preferred not to wake up in the middle of the night to a torrential rainfall, soaked to the bones.

Carson suggested their camouflage would be enough to hide them once dark, meaning they didn't need to take shifts keeping watch and while Tyler agreed, a part of him couldn't put to rest the anxiety that had begun once he'd laid eyes on the complex.

As the daylight faded and the darkness enveloped everything, Carson positioned himself against the tree boughs. Tyler knew that Carson felt protective of him. Whether it was due to occupation, age or a natural trait, Tyler was glad for it. It gave him a sense of relief and he saw Carson filling the place that Neil normally took. Tyler couldn't count the number of times over the years that he'd experienced severe fear, to the point of tears, from various places they'd hiked or camped. His dad had always been there, always reassured him and told him he was there, that he wouldn't let anything happen to him.

Tyler saw that Carson was exhausted, watching the cop fall asleep in the blink of an eye. *Must be nice,* he thought. Carson whimpered as he slept, Tyler knowing that he was already dreaming. He closed his eyes, entering his own dream state just as fast as Carson.

He was watching his mom and dad in this dream.

It was a strange experience, to see his parents together, hiking through the woods. He could see two soldiers watching his parents.

They followed from a distance, making sure they stayed in the shadows, always out of sight. His parents were walking at a slower pace than Tyler thought they would've, the reason finally showing itself when they stopped for a drink. As his mom turned, her protruding belly came into view.

I'm in there, Tyler thought.

When his parents continued, so did the soldiers. Tyler wasn't in control, not in the dream, but he understood this was a good thing. If he had any ability to manipulate the situation, he'd attempt to warn his parents, speak to them, tell them to run and get away.

He was so lost in thought over what he'd do if he had the chance that he hadn't noticed they'd come to a halt. Looking at his parents, he saw his mother was holding her stomach, pain flashing across her face.

There, gone, there, gone.

Contractions.

His dad was moving frantically. Tyler didn't know how else to process what he was watching. His dad helped his mom to the ground and laid a blanket down at the same time. Grabbing a sleeping bag he placed it under her head. Once done, he got a fire going and put a pot of water on to start boiling. His father was a man possessed, knowing an intricate game plan of what needed to be done, in what order and when. It made Tyler smile. His dad had always been a man of meticulous preparation. While at home he was easy going and playful, but once they started to prepare for a hiking trip or even when he would be leaving for work for more than a week, he had a game plan set up. They went over each detail, not once, not twice, but as many times as needed and they covered *everything.*

Tyler couldn't help but see just how excited his dad had been for his arrival. It didn't matter that their baby was arriving in the wilderness. Those two loved the outdoors so much that Neil had made sure he could handle this situation should the moment arrive.

Once again, Tyler was lost in thought, not paying attention to what was unfolding.

This can't actually be what happened, can it?

The two soldiers were moving forwards, first at a normal pace, and then they were jogging.

Tyler could see the crown of his own head followed by his shoulders, arms and then his body flopped out. His dad wrapped him in a blanket, and just as Tyler let out his first cry into the world, the two men raised their guns, the silencers doing their jobs.

Tyler jolted awake, his eyes searching, his brain struggling to figure out where he was. The vividness of the dream had left a cut through his soul, but once he remembered that he was in the lean-to with Carson and that none of that had actually happened, he calmed.

Beside him, Carson still whimpered.

Tyler reached out to give him a push, try to wake him from whatever horrible dream he was experiencing, when a thick huff was let out mere feet from their structure.

Our dreams caused us to make sounds, Tyler thought. *They attracted something.*

Either that or their old friend the lizard-creature had tracked them down and was here to finish them off.

Tyler knew he needed Carson to wake up and stop whimpering, but he didn't want to startle him awake and cause an attack if Carson spoke, unaware of the imminent danger.

The unseen visitor shifted, and from the way the air moved and the ground appeared to cave in around the base of their shelter, Tyler knew it was massive.

Wasn't every beast here, though?

"Carson," he whispered, trying his best not to alert whatever it was outside. The man didn't shift, but he did let out a murmur.

Tyler knew he needed to keep him quiet.

He lunged over and covered Carson's mouth with his hands, watching as his eyes flew open. He put a finger to his lips, trying to get Carson to see it was just him, just Tyler trying to keep them alive.

From outside another huff came, this one wetter and deeper. That got Carson's attention.

He sat up and they moved back against the dirt wall.

"What the fuck is that?" Carson whispered.

Tyler shrugged his shoulders. He held one hand as high as he could, then held both hands as wide as he could. Carson caught on; the thing was huge.

Carson then held up a hand and moved it in a slithering fashion.

Is it the lizard?

Tyler shook his head. While he couldn't say with absolute certainty, Tyler didn't believe it was the lizard.

The two stared at the dark boughs before them, not sure what to do next.

As they sat silently, a new sound joined the heavy breathing from outside; the patter of rain.

Just great, Tyler thought.

As the rain increased in intensity, thunder sounded, followed shortly by lightning.

The storm was close.

The rain fell, the thunder boomed and lightning flashed.

Only this time, when the lightning flashed, it created a silhouette through the boughs.

Both of them cringed seeing the massive shape of the beast just feet away from them.

With the next crack of lightning, the beast's outline was closer, looking even larger.

They needed to move, but how? The beast was as wide as their lean-to, blocking the way for them to make their escape.

Before they could even think of a possible plan, the thunder boomed, the lightning crashed, and the beast exploded forward.

30

An implosion of shrapnel and splintered wood slammed into the two as the beast crashed through the branches and careened into the dirt wall behind them. Carson and Tyler leapt to the side, narrowly avoiding being crushed by the creature or impaled by the debris.

Carson got to his feet, moving away, wanting to put distance between himself and the rampaging abomination. Tyler wasn't so lucky, and found that where he'd jumped had trapped him between a rock and the roots of a downed tree. He looked left and right, trying to find an escape route before the thing discovered him. It was still pawing and slamming its claws into where the two were previously.

Tyler began pulling himself up the roots, thinking this was his only option to flee. He got halfway up when he heard a noise and, looking over his shoulder, saw the beast's single eye was now locked on him.

He tried to scramble faster, but the beast lashed out with a paw. Fortunately, it connected more with the roots than directly with Tyler, but the impact still sent him flying. He landed with a hard thud, the air knocked from his lungs.

Before he even had a chance to stand, Carson was beside him. He hooked an arm around Tyler and pulled him to his feet, then began to drag him towards a bulky downed tree. The inside had all but rotten away, allowing the two men to tumble into the interior. They could hear the beast tromping around near them, but for whatever reason it hadn't followed them, nor was it attempting to crash through the tree.

Maybe it didn't see where we went? Tyler thought, its one eye possibly limiting what it could see or how far. He wasn't sure and he wasn't about to pop out of their refuge and ask the beast.

They remained where they were while the rain continued to fall with tremendous force, the collective volume enough to begin a shallow flood inside the tree. Their feet were submerged in a few inches by the time the creature rumbled away. They didn't fully trust that it had left, Carson whispering to Tyler to be careful and not make any sounds in case it was setting a trap.

So, they sat and waited.

31

"I think we're good," Tyler said.

The two left the soaked refuge, nervously looking around. Both expected something to come rampaging towards them from the depths of the trees.

"Look at that," Carson said, pointing at their former shelter.

It was in shambles. The beast had made sure to give it a proper battering, the branches and logs used to create it lying decimated.

"You think our stuff survived?" Carson asked.

Tyler walked to where his pack had been and after pulling aside some branches, found it sitting right where he'd left it, somehow untouched.

Carson let out a whoop as he found his pack was also unscathed.

"How the hell did that happen?"

"I don't know man, but I'm glad it did," Carson replied.

"Let's consider it another good sign. We have our mystery 'bellower' who has helped guide us, and now somehow our gear wasn't destroyed when a five-thousand-pound, one-eyed behemoth crushed everything else," Tyler said.

"And nearly crushed you," Carson said.

"And nearly crushed me. That's true. The only bumps I got are on my ass, which shouldn't be an issue," Tyler said, both of them laughing.

They slung their packs over their shoulders and turned towards their destination.

The complex loomed large in their minds, sitting just hours away.

As they made their way through the dense forest, moving ever closer to the structure, they both had different images of just what awaited them.

Carson appeared more sullen than normal. Tyler couldn't read what was going on inside his head, but he knew a battle was being fought. He suspected most of what Carson was grappling over was whether his dad was still alive and just what they'd have to do if he was.

It was a daunting thing to process, especially when you took into consideration just how difficult it had been to arrive at this very place.

No matter what they discovered, no matter what the ultimate outcome of their arrival at the complex would be, they'd need to make their way *back* out of this valley. Back to the perimeter, down the paths, to the vehicles and even after that – another hour drive to the town.

And who would that be? Returning? Tyler didn't want to put any thought into who might still be alive. Or might not.

Now his brain was on overdrive and he started to think about the possible conditions if they were alive. Dehydrated? Emaciated? Just what state would his dad be in if they did find him? The entire scenario that rattled around through Tyler's head was overwhelming to a level he'd never believed possible. But there was no turning back now. No quitting. Not for him, at least. He didn't believe Carson would quit, not at this stage, but Tyler needed to keep it in the back of his mind that he may end up alone or it just may be him and Neil. Tyler wasn't a big guy, a strong guy, so the idea of having to haul his dad back over miles and miles of inhospitable wilderness peppered with clearings that had killing spikes and insane beast's roaming the valley brought on another bout of impending panic.

Calm. Calm, he told himself.

"What's going to be the first thing you do when we get back to the *real* world?" Carson asked, breaking Tyler's escalating thoughts.

"Probably see if I graduated," Tyler replied, causing Carson to laugh.

"Seriously?"

"Seriously. What about you?"

"Think I might take a drive to Vancouver. Just be a tourist for a week. See a concert, or rent a helicopter and go on a tour," Carson said.

"My dad has a friend who does plane tours up in Squamish. You could go do that. David's a great guy," Tyler said.

"That would be something I'd love to do. You travel much?"

"Yeah. Dad and I have been all over, hiking and camping. Alaska, Yukon, Manitoba, Quebec, Scotland, Spain, through a bunch of Europe, China, Russia, some parts of South America. My dad always said we were born to walk the Earth and he took that literally," Tyler said, finding he was getting emotional thinking about all of their adventures.

"That's great. I never travelled much. Hell, my dad was the town cop, so he was always on duty. Then like a stubborn fool, I became the town cop. And even though there's five of us working the station, I'm my dad's son, you know? So, most of the time folks still call me or come by the house if they know I'm not on shift. The other members all came from across Canada, so to many of the townspeople, they're foreigners," Carson said, letting out a laugh that was filled with sadness.

Tyler just nodded. He couldn't imagine being a cop, let alone the son of a cop. Especially in a small town.

"So, have you never been across Canada or anything?"

"Nope. I did my training in Regina, and that's the farthest East I've been. Fuck, I haven't even been to the States. One of my old girlfriend's always said we should go to Vegas. She practically begged me to travel there, but the guilt I felt over leaving the town, even for the weekend, was too much. I never went. She did. With her next boyfriend. They're actually married now."

Tyler knew the tone of their talk was starting to change. If it kept getting darker, Carson would get locked into his despair and they'd never recover.

"So, go. You know what, I'll go with you. We'll hit the strip, play some cards, and see some topless ladies."

"Ha! Well, that's very kind of you, but you wouldn't be old enough for most of what you just suggested down there."

"True. I'll stand outside and keep your wallet safe."

They both had smiles on their faces, which was what Tyler had hoped to accomplish.

They settled into their rhythm again. Similar to Neil and Tyler's but different.

Footsteps and silence, observing the wilderness around them.

The complex could now be seen through the trees ahead.

32

———

Two summers ago, Neil and Tyler decided to make the journey down to Mount St. Helens. They'd always wanted to hike the area and see what had become of the landscape after the eruption that happened in May, 1980.

Neil had told Tyler about living through that time. How the sky had darkened, and how, even where they lived in the Lower Mainland, ash had rained down.

Tyler couldn't fathom it. A volcano had *actually* erupted in the United States. He'd always thought of that only happening across the Atlantic or the Pacific Ocean. Somewhere *over there*, far away when you found it on the map.

They'd parked and hiked in, planning to spend as much of the day as they could being geology nerds. Trying to find discarded volcanic rock and scorch marks on deadfall. While they were mostly out of luck finding anything to bring home with them, one thing that they wouldn't forget was the sheer magnitude of the event.

It left Tyler shaken, knowing that something that big had happened so close.

Now, as he and Carson arrived at the perimeter fence

that zig-zagged through the trees on this side of the complex, Tyler was once again left with the sense that they'd underestimated the dimensions of this military compound. The fence alone was at least forty feet tall and the razor wire that looped along the top was frightening, even from where they stood hidden in the trees.

The guard tower nearest them was a square shaped room on top of a circular cement stack. An enclosed walkway travelled from the back of the structure leading to the main complex area behind it. Looking at the base they didn't see any obvious cameras and the windows that filled three of the outer walls were dark, which they both assumed meant they were currently unmanned. A stroke of luck on their part, but Tyler also wondered if it was too convenient.

"There's an emergency access ladder," Carson said, pointing to it. "There's one on either side of the fence. I know how to get into their hatches, once we get up. This part will be stressful, but we need to climb that ladder as fast as we can and get in before someone on patrol comes around."

"Doesn't it seem a bit easy?" Tyler asked. "Like, we're just going to go up the ladder and in?"

"This place doesn't get people breaking in. This complex is designed to keep things inside, Tyler, but the fence would be used purely to slow down any creatures that wander this way. Never in a million years are they believing a person would not only somehow get across the basin and arrive here, surviving the trip, but would then voluntarily want to break into this complex."

Tyler knew Carson was right. This wasn't a bank protecting billions of dollars on a street corner.

Taking one more look to make sure they were still alone, Carson ran from the trees across the short clearing to the base of the ladder. Tyler hadn't even thought of the narrow section being booby trapped like the other clearings until it was too late, but it didn't matter. Carson wasn't blown apart by hidden spikes that burst from the ground. Tyler followed and arrived just as Carson was beginning the climb.

With each additional rung up the ladder, Tyler expected alarms to sound, spotlights to focus on them and for rabid attack dogs to begin barking and snarling from below. Surprisingly, none of that happened.

Carson arrived at the hatch, and before Tyler could even ask Carson how he was going to open it, a popping noise sounded like a seal opening for the first time and the entrance door flopped up and into the space.

Pushing his head through, Carson found that they'd been correct. Nobody was in the tower. He didn't believe they'd have long before whoever was supposed to be here would return. They might simply be on a perimeter sweep or a systems check. Carson was treating this place like a maximum-security prison, which Tyler thought worked for the best, especially if they wanted to remain out of sight for as long as possible.

"We need to move," Carson said, extending a hand to help pull Tyler into the room. The area was set up similarly to the monitoring stations in the woods. The biggest difference here was that the station was usable and active. The screens were on, with some showing the trees around the fences. *There* are *cameras*, Tyler thought. Others had images of hallways, while some were displaying the area outside of the complex, with several parked Jeeps. Tyler looked through the angled windows, back into the forest they'd come from. A part of him realized he was looking for any sign of his mystery guide.

From the outside it had been a covered walkway, but

within the guard tower, Tyler and Carson found it was a nondescript hallway leading back into the main building. Looking through the window of the door that entered into the hallway, they saw the area was clear. Carson still pushed the door open slowly before they started towards the complex. They'd only taken a few steps when Tyler stopped.

"Carson, look at us. We're wearing our regular clothes. Someone will notice us, either on a camera or from a distance. We need to find something so we can blend in."

Returning to the guard room, they frantically searched the cabinets that filled a back corner before finding some infantry suits hanging in the third cabinet. Tyler tossed one to Carson and grabbed one for himself, which they both hurried to put on. Another cabinet revealed darkened glasses and fabric face masks, which they also put on.

Now, confidently disguised, they re-entered the hallway.

Upon first glance, the building had a similar lay-out to most hospitals. Levels made up of rooms and labs. Tyler tried his best to not look through most of the windows, but from time to time, movement would catch his eye and his curiosity got the best of him. In some, he saw soldiers in hospital beds. Some had blisters and bandages as though they'd suffered radiation burns, while others looked to be recovering from surgery. The further along they went the odder the subjects in the rooms became, where soon even Carson was taking longer and longer looks. There were animals in cages, infants in clear bassinets, and scientists in lab coats busy looking in microscopes.

"The more things I see in these rooms, the worse the dread I feel growing gets."

Tyler understood. Things were *off*.

At the end of the hallway, they came to an exit door presumably leading to the stairwell.

"What's our game plan here? I feel like we're blindly sprinting with absolutely no sense of reason or purpose? The size of this place alone would take us weeks, if not months, to inspect each room on each level. We're risking being found with every passing moment."

"You're right. I don't think we should, be we would cover more ground by splitting up. What do you think?" Carson said.

Tyler looked at Carson then back down the way they'd just come. It was the logical choice but also the most irrational one. Neither had any sort of weapon. Carson was trained to subdue an attacker; Tyler had no self-defense training to speak of. But there was a chance his dad was in this building and Tyler knew they were running on decreasing borrowed time.

"OK. Let's do that. I'll go up, you go down. How about thirty minutes and we meet back here. If one of us gets here and the other isn't – no hesitation, we go searching for the other, agreed?"

Carson agreed. They synchronized their watches, each setting an alarm for thirty minutes.

"Good luck, stay safe," Carson said, pushing the button on his watch to start the countdown.

"Same," Tyler replied, as he turned and pushed open the door to the stairwell.

He let Carson go into the stairwell first. His friend didn't look back as he went down the stairs.

Tyler didn't wait long after Carson left, taking the steps up two at a time before he arrived at the next landing. He took a breath and went to open the door, when it was pulled away and a man in a lab coat pushed by.

"Sorry, soldier," the man said, as he hustled past, not even bothering to look at Tyler. He didn't even have time to respond, but felt it was probably for the best. If the man didn't recognize his voice, he'd immediately become suspicious. Of course, Tyler wasn't sure just how many people worked at this building and the chances that the man would recognize each person's voice was slim.

Stepping into the hallway, Tyler found this level appeared to be an exact replica of the previous. He hoped that the contents of each room were different, though.

He wasn't completely sure he wanted to see what atrocities he might discover on this level, but he needed to.

His dad needed him to.

He wished, somehow, that his guiding animal would let out a bellow and tell him where to go. He never should've separated from Carson, this much he knew. Alone now, on this level and with no safety net, it took everything in him not to turn and run back the way he'd come, down the stairs to the level that Carson would be searching.

33

WHEN THEY SPLIT UP, CARSON DECIDED TO HEAD TO THE basement and work his way back up. He knew it would take longer than thirty minutes, but he didn't care. This was his one chance to find his dad and if it meant that Tyler would need to come looking for him, so be it.

When he arrived at the bottom, he'd lost count of how many levels it had been. At least a dozen if not more.

The door that awaited him was different from the others. The handle was thicker, the frame reinforced, the door itself looked heavier. He grabbed the handle and pushed, finding more resistance than expected. He leaned into it and worked his feet into the floor. He could feel the soles of his boots wanting to slide under him, the slick concrete not allowing him to find any grip. Then, slowly, the door began to move. Carson continued to push, continued to struggle, until finally he'd opened up enough space for him to slip through.

The hallway he entered was dark. As he took a few steps into the space, a buzzing sounded and fluorescent strips of lighting flickered to life above him, illuminating the span.

The level was similar in layout to the upper levels, but it had subtle differences. Instead of standard flooring, it was covered in a rug that travelled the length of the space. There were fancy lighting sconces at even intervals along the walls and where the lab windows were located a leather reclining chair sat facing the window.

Just what in the fuck is in each room that you'd want to sit and watch?

Carson felt compelled to move forward. He knew he didn't want to, but it was as though some unseen force latched onto his center of gravity and his body had to either follow or fall over.

At the first window the interior was lit up. Stepping behind the chair, he looked in and was surprised to find it empty.

"Welcome," a female voice spoke from an unseen speaker and Carson jumped, looking frantically around.

"Jesus Christ," he said, not seeing anyone or where the voice had come from.

"Hello and welcome, customer. Your payment has not been processed yet. Please be aware we will need to see you at administration following your experience. Is that acceptable?"

Carson stood silently, not sure what was going on, or if he was supposed to respond.

"Is that acceptable?" the woman repeated.

"Uh, yeah. Yes," he replied.

"Very well. Please have a seat and await further instructions."

Carson looked around again, still unsure of what he'd stumbled on. All of his police instincts told him he should turn and leave, find Tyler and get the hell out of here, but the idea of potentially being so close to his dad lingered.

What if he left now and his dad was just through that door at the end of the hallway?

So, he sat.

The chair was possibly the most comfortable piece of furniture he'd ever been on. The leather was divine, the cushioning perfect.

It was then that the weight of their journey and the lack of sleep really caught up. He could sense that he was drifting closer and closer to sleepville. Thankfully, the female voice returned.

"First selection please, customer. Fight or fuck?"

"What?"

"First selection please, customer. Fight or fuck?"

"Uh, shit, uh fight?"

"Very well."

The room before him transformed from fluorescent to a red-tinged light.

Two square sections of the floor slid open, one on either side of the room. Carson sat up straighter, trying to see what was below, but before he could get a clear view, a cage rose in each opening.

"What the fuck?"

Monstrosities.

That's the closest word that could describe the inhabitants of each cage.

The figure on Carson's left had the anatomy of a human from the waist down; human legs, a penis and testicles. Its feet were misshapen as though they'd undergone numerous surgical procedures, but for the most part they looked like human feet. The torso was closer to that of an animal, dark fur covering their chest and back. One arm was human from the shoulder to the elbow, while the forearm and hand were instead either wood or rock. From where he sat, Carson couldn't be positive. The other arm was a lobster claw, the figure's shoulder to where the claw started was a thick red armored appendage. The figure's face was hard to define. Carson could make out a mouth, with one side almost human, the other side sloughing off into rubbery skin that hung down a good foot from its jaw. It was either a cyclops or the other eye was buried somewhere in a fold.

All told, the thing standing there made Carson want to puke.

Did he dare look to his right? He knew he had to. The abomination that greeted his eyes made him stand up, tears springing uncontrollably forward.

Another grotesque creation stood hunched over in the cage, but even with the bars limiting some of his view, Carson knew who it was immediately.

His dad. Or some test tube version.

His arms were no longer human. Both were matted in dark, sticky fur and ended with gigantic bear paws. The claws that tipped each pad were rounded and dulled, but still thick enough that they'd cause some serious damage should they connect with flesh. Carson took a step towards the window, his movement catching the attention of the beast he wished to God wasn't who it was.

"Son?" the thing managed to choke out when recognition dawned on him, the voice no longer the voice Carson heard when remembering conversations they'd shared.

"Dad?"

"The customer has chosen Fight," the woman spoke, breaking the momentary spell father and son had been under.

It all clicked into place and Carson realized what the purpose of this level was. Depraved souls, those with money, would pay to come down here and watch these experiments 'fight or fuck.' He rushed to the glass, slamming it with his hands, trying to smash it. Before him the lobster figure advanced. Every part of him knew his dad had no chance in this fight. Even as his dad lashed out and lunged with his claws, the lobster-man blocked the strikes with its armored crustacean appendage and, with one swift downward blow, bashed his dad in the face, removing more than half of it. Seeing the damage incurred by the strike, Carson understood the figure possessed an arm of stone. As he stood helplessly, he watched as the lobster-man pummeled his dad's skull over and over again, until it was just a pulpy mush.

"No!" He screamed and clawed at the glass, desperately searching his brain for a way to turn back time. He sunk down, legs no longer able to hold him, coming to a stop on the floor, sobbing into his hands. A tapping behind him got his attention and turning, looked at the glass. The lobster-man was tapping its claw, glaring at Carson.

It raised its lobster arm, snapping the two long pincers together as it did. Then it pulled it across its neck in a slicing action. The gesture was a familiar one to the cop, although the 'slit-throat' motion wasn't one he often had to deal with in such a small town.

"Customer, the event has concluded. Would you like to purchase another viewing for section two?"

The female voice took him away from the monster behind the glass. He didn't want to continue on. The remains of his father, the man he'd been searching for, for so many years, lay a dozen feet from him. How could this have been the ending?

"Customer?"

He wiped his face, the tears still coming. He looked once more for cameras but still found no obvious sign of where they were embedded or hidden. He knew someone, somewhere was watching him.

"Yes," he answered, starting towards the second chair. He stopped, looking back towards where his dad lay, ignoring the aggressive movements the lobster-man continued to direct towards him.

When he couldn't look any longer, he went to the second chair. This room was the same as the first. Empty until he decided what carnage would be unleashed.

"Please sit, customer."

Unless the system was completely automated and motion activated, Carson was confident he was being watched and that whoever was in charge had been alerted that an unexpected visitor was in a paying area. He looked for a possible escape route, something other than the door he'd come through or the exit that was somewhere further ahead beyond where the light reached.

"Please sit, customer," the female repeated.

Carson hesitated. His dad was still bashed into a mess a dozen feet from him. But his professional side took over. *What else was happening here?*

I'll mourn him once we get out, he thought, wondering briefly how Tyler was doing.

Carson reluctantly sat, finding this recliner to be every bit as comfortable as the last. Before he could shift metal clamps extended from the armrests and from the bottom of the chair around his wrists and ankles, locking him with a loud *click* in place.

"Hey! Hey!" He yelled out, but to no avail.

"Customer, please make a selection. Fuck or fry?"

Oh Jesus, he thought.

"Fry, I choose fry," he said, bitterly.

"Customer has selected Fry," the female said, before a

beeping noise began. Carson cringed at the same sound that drew animals into the killing clearings.

From the center of the room a metallic pole appeared from below the floor, extending almost to the height of the ceiling. The beeping intensified from the pole. Instead of cages arriving from openings in the floor, three doors opened from the back wall, from which three human figures were pushed into view, two women and one man, each person nude. The doors slammed shut once they were fully in the room. Each had a dark strip covering their eyes, their arms outstretched trying to figure out where they were. Carson could see the thick scars and weeping wounds that covered their bodies. Bound to the chair, he was unable to move away from what was about to happen. He had a desire to turn his head away, to look anywhere else, but a primal, repulsive part of him was curious to see how they'd make out. The beeping intensified but with the wrist cuffs tightly in place, Carson was unable to cover his ears. The figures stumbled around in the space, blindfolds ensuring that not even a sliver of light could be seen by the person. It was only a matter of time until one of them made contact, but when the woman collided with the taller of the two men, she bounced off him and hit the pole. Carson could hear her scream through the glass. She didn't stop moving forward. From where he sat, it looked as though the pole was a human magnet, a force pulling her against her will. She took another step as the pole seared through her like a hot knife through butter. One half of her flopped to her left, the other to the right. The two men were now within the unseen force and a similar fate met them, as they howled in agony as the pole split each of them in half.

Even split in two, Carson knew their pain wasn't over.

Nerves were still firing, even to a now dead system, and their legs and arms kicked and flopped for a few more seconds.

"Customer, you have been approved to view room three for free."

"I don't want to. Thank you, but I'm fine," he said, knowing it most likely didn't matter what he wanted.

"Customer, you successfully sat through all three bisections. Credit has been extended for room three. Please make your way to the third viewing seat."

The shackles unclasped and retracted, his wrists and ankles released. He stood, rubbing where the metal had dug into his forearms, before grudgingly proceeding to the third chair. There was a side table that was previously unseen, the recliner blocking it from view. On the table sat a box of tissues and a pump bottle of lotion.

"Good Christ," Carson said.

"Customer, please make a selection, Fuck or fuck."

"What?"

"Customer, please make a selection, Fuck or fuck."

Carson did not want to see any more of this freak show. But this was the last room. *Watch this, then get through that final door and go and find Tyler.*

"Fuck," he said, not as a reply but in anger.

"The customer has selected Fuck. Please enjoy."

34

Tyler searched the level with such haste he was nearly running. He needed to find his dad before he himself was discovered. Now that he was on his own, each level appeared as though it was staffed by more and more people. It created a fear bubbling just below his paranoia.

The first level he searched on his own was a near replica of the one below. Labs, beds, tables, all sterile environments for medical people to do their work.

As he continued up, he found these levels were changing from medical and moving towards administrative. One side of the hallway was the same. Large windows looking into a research area. The other side though no longer had windows to peer through. Instead it was made up of closed doors. Each door had a number and a name on it, but it meant nothing to Tyler. Where a hospital might have stated *'Dr. Thompson,'* the first one he looked at said *'H-13223.'* Whether that was some sort of military code or even an experiment chart number, he'd never know.

Without any idea of his dad's location in the complex, he couldn't use that system of door labelling for any use. So he kept going, spending his time looking for anything in the lab rooms that would point him in the correct direction.

Reaching the end of the hallway, Tyler heard a door opening. He froze at the stairwell door, looking back to see who'd exited their office.

Two men stepped out, both wearing white lab coats. One looked to be a few decades older than the other man and for a brief moment Tyler wondered if they were father and son, the similarities between the two striking.

"I've run the numbers. H-55443 just isn't ready for optimization yet, Greg. I mean, we could theoretically see how it would survive in the valley, but I think the blades would destroy it by day's end," the older man said.

"You never have faith in my results, but that's fine," the younger man said, raising his hands. "I get it, you don't want any of my stuff to look good or otherwise they'll toss your old ass into the woods."

They both laughed, walking the opposite way from Tyler down the hall.

"Look," the older man said, "let's send H-55443 to Afghanistan or hell, Russia, for all I care. Somewhere that if shit goes tits up, the government will have to clean up the mess and it won't be us having to do hours of paperwork during unpaid overtime."

"Fuck. I hadn't thought of that. O'Hallahan asked if I had any projects I could send overseas. That's a great idea, I'll catch up later, I'm gonna see if that old Irish prick is still looking for volunteers."

Tyler waited until the older man entered a room and the younger man stepped into the stairwell. Having not been spotted by them, he felt invigorated, as though his presence blended in. He went up to the next level, wondering if he'd end up running into the man in the lab coat. Tyler had no way of knowing what level the man had planned on going to, but it could very well have been this one.

Exiting the stairwell into the hall, Tyler didn't find the man, but he did see a woman sitting in the hallway. She had a cup of coffee beside her, flipping through some papers. She wore dress pants and a button up shirt and Tyler almost laughed at the absurdity of the scenario. To her, this complex was normal, routine. Business as usual. Her workplace, where her colleagues were friends and every day was just another day at the office. Tyler tried to return into the stairwell without disturbing her, when he thought he heard her speak.

Turning back, he saw that she was standing and looking at him.

"Pardon?"

"I said, why are you on this floor, soldier? Let me see your papers and your ID number."

Before Tyler could think of a reply, she'd closed the distance and was now standing uncomfortably close.

"What is this? You're just a child? Are we so hard up for bodies now, that they're recruiting high schoolers?"

Tyler didn't know what to say. Instead he remained silent, watching her run through some internal scenarios, hoping maybe she'd send him on his way.

"Well? Are you deaf? Papers and ID number," she said, holding out her hand.

Tyler feigned looking for them, patting his pockets and shoulders, feeling completely foolish but trying to figure a way out of this.

"You do know the punishment for entering an off-limits level without official papers, don't you?"

Tyler shook his head. This wasn't good.

"Death. Are you new here?"

"Yes," he said, his throat the driest it had ever been. "First day."

"Oh, well. Lucky you came across me then. Why are you up here?"

Tyler decided to give it a shot. He had nothing else to lose.

"I'm supposed to find the location of a subject. A... uh... Neil Barton and report back."

"Who ordered it?"

"Uh... Doctor Neb... uh, I'm sorry, I can't remember his name. It was on the papers, which are sitting with my ID."

"That's fine, follow me. I'll pull up the database."

He waited until she turned and walked, putting some distance between the two of them. Sweat poured down his sides like bullets. He was sure this wouldn't work, but she seemed friendly enough.

She went into the office beside where he'd found her sitting, and closed the door once they'd entered. He was surprised at how big the space was. While she went to her computer and started to log in, he looked at the walls, hoping to find more details that would help him and Carson. The wall nearest him was covered in degrees, awards and newspaper articles, all praising the woman. Dr. Cynthia Meddle. Once he was back home, he'd need to remember her name and search online, see what she'd done to end up here. He didn't find any personal photos. Everything had a military sterility to it.

His eyes went from wall to wall, ending on the aerial map of the entire basin that covered the space directly behind her. The detail of it was staggering. He could see rivers, roads, and buildings. His eagerness caught her attention.

"See something you like?" she asked. Tyler wasn't too

thrilled with the tone of her voice. Accusing more than anything.

"No, Dr. Meddle, just never seen it like that before."

"You know my name?"

He pointed to the wall of accolades sheepishly, which resulted in her laughing.

"Good point. Hard to miss who I am. I'm just teasing. God, you new ones are always strung so tight. Must be those marches they force you to take."

She turned her attention back to the screen, her hand moving the mouse and clicking, moving and clicking. As much as he wanted to move around behind the desk to watch her search, he knew that would be over the line, even with her joking nature.

"Ah, here we go. Neil Barton. H-55443. Interesting. This was from the plane that was shot down a few days back. Huh? They really sped up his processing timeline. What info did you need, soldier?"

They'd shot down the plane? They'd shot down the plane.

He was shaking. The room spun; his chest felt heavy. The two men in the hallway had discussed sending H-55443 to Afghanistan or Russia. The man had hurried away to make sure they could still send that subject. That subject was his dad. *Jesus Christ. His dad.*

"You alright there, newbie?" She asked it, without taking her eyes from the screen, not seeing the change in him. "Hmm, that's strange. Ultra-high clearance on this subject. Looks like he was targeted. Luckily for you, you stumbled into the right woman today; I have full clearance. *And* I didn't kill you when you couldn't show me your papers or ID. Let's see."

If Dr. Meddle had looked at him instead of remaining focused on the screen, she would've seen Tyler turning as pale as a ghost and his eyeballs roll back in his head. His knees buckled and when he hit the floor of her office, she jumped in surprise.

"Oh shit, are you OK?"

She rushed around the desk, relieved to hear a low moan escape his lips. His eyes fluttered as he returned to full consciousness, and with her assistance Tyler got himself back to a sitting position.

"You sure you picked the right career path?"

He tried to force a smile, but nothing would come.

"What brought that on?"

She returned to the desk without waiting for an answer. His legs felt unsteady as he stood but when she spoke again, alarm bells sounded in his head.

"Helmet off, soldier."

It was an order. It wasn't a kind request, or a suggestion to help him feel better after his fall. This was a direct order that he knew he needed to follow.

He unclipped the chin strap and removed the helmet, holding it in his hands in front of his stomach.

"Tyler Barton? Correct?"

Discovered. The file she had open on the computer would've contained a photo of him. How he'd been so care-less, so reckless and absent minded about that was beyond him. But it wasn't. He was exhausted, desperate to find his dad and achingly close.

They met eyes. He believed if she had a gun, he'd be dead already.

"Yes, Dr. Meddle."

"Just how in the hell did you make it in here? And why are you here?"

His eyes darted to the door. Back to her. To the door. *Where was Carson?*

"My finger's on the alarm button, Tyler. Don't make me push it. Answer me and maybe we can figure some shit out."

"I just want to find my dad. I know he survived the plane crash."

She nodded, eyes glancing at the screen, something registering that she hadn't caught before.

"Shit. Your mom's here as well?"

"She's alive?"

Tyler couldn't believe it. *Confirmation.* Both of his parents were here *and* alive.

"I gotta say, Tyler. I'm actually impressed. You're the first person to make it from perimeter to base. We've had stragglers before, but usually something picks them off easily enough. Or they get to the wall and can't figure out a way past. But you, you did it."

Tyler couldn't be sure, but a look of respect appeared to cross her face for the briefest of moments.

"Look, kid. I know this sucks, and I do feel for you, but I can't let you go. You know that right?"

She clicked the mouse a couple more times, the printer making a zipping sound as something printed out.

"Here," she said, holding the sheet out. "Take it."

He took the paper and looked at it.

"That is the last photo of your mom uploaded on her patient chart. I'm sorry. It doesn't look like much of her has remained."

She was right. Tyler had a stabbing pain in his stomach when he looked at the page, but Dr. Meddle was right.

He recognized the human half of her face from their old photos. Even the way her lips curved up. Whatever it was covering the rest of her was indistinguishable and the mossy tree growths that sprouted from everywhere made him rush to the waste basket beside her desk and puke in painful, sobbing heaves.

"Why?" he said, wiping wet remains from his lips and chin.

She stood and approached, keeping her distance.

"Science. Evolution. Achievement. Military power. What do you want me to say?"

"I just wanted my mom. Do you know what that was like? To lose her but to never have her? To only know her face from photos. I don't even know what her voice sounds like. Or her touch. And now I find out you took my dad to do the same? I didn't deserve this. She didn't. He didn't. None of us did. Growing up, every single birthday and Christmas I wished for my mom to come back."

Dr. Meddle went to reply, but before she got the first word out, Tyler reared back and delivered a straight cross to her chin. She went down hard. He checked to see if she had a pulse or not and, finding one, he stuffed the photo into a pocket, then went to the door. With a hard kick, he busted the handle off from the inside and closed it behind him, leaving her in a heap on the floor. After confirming it wouldn't open from the outside, he ran to the stairwell at the end of the hall.

He needed to find Carson before she woke up.

35

Carson wished he had battery acid to splash on his eyes.

Two human-beast hybrids were pushed into the room and started grinding against each other before Carson could look away.

He'd rather be looking at his father's remains than this macabre play. Anything to have this end would be better than what was happening a dozen feet away.

Parts inserted, grotesque squeals sounded and fluid splashed and before he knew it, one beast had ripped the head off the other.

It let out a climactic roar as it slurped on the contents of the severed head. Carson had had enough but knew he couldn't just leave. He sat, waiting for the voice to speak.

"Customer, we hope your expectations were met. Please exit and proceed to the cashier. An encrypted email will be sent in the next few days. Please do leave us a review for future purchasers."

The sound of locks disengaging occurred, followed by the door releasing. Carson pushed the heavy thing open and stepped into a lobby.

It was as though he'd entered an entirely new world.

An expansive gold desk sat nestled into a corner. A man in a tailored suit sat behind the desk, busy on the computer. Three leather couches were positioned around a gas fireplace, flames dancing along the insert.

Light jazz was playing from hidden speakers and a woman stood silently in the corner, holding a tray of drinks. As soon as she spotted Carson, she hustled over and offered him a flute of champagne. He declined with the wave of his hand while looking for the exit.

"Ah, soldier. Come, we need to settle up your account," the man called from behind the desk. "I presume all was to your liking?"

Carson sat, staring at the man across from him, not offering a reply.

"Papers and badge please," the man asked with a mild tone of annoyance.

"Don't have them."

The man adjusted his glasses, blinking frantically.

"Papers and badge please," he repeated.

Carson held up his hands to show they were empty.

"Sorry," he said.

"Well, this is unheard of. Who approved this?"

Carson shrugged, enjoying how much he was getting under this man's skin.

"Let's try this a different way. Unit and location."

"Don't know," Carson replied.

"This is unacceptable. Unacceptable."

The man was muttering to himself, while he opened and closed drawers of the desk at random. Carson could see he'd completely unhinged the man.

Deciding he didn't want to wait any longer, Carson stood and headed towards the door.

"Take another step and I'm calling security."

Carson stopped, looking at the man who was now standing at the desk, phone receiver in hand.

"I need to go get my papers. Right?"

The man started to speak, but Carson cut him off.

"Look, I'm new. I didn't know the protocols. Our group leader told me to come, blow off some steam. So, I came down. I'm sorry. Let me go grab them and I'll come right back. How much do I owe?"

The man hesitantly sat and looked at the computer screen.

"Let's see... You sat through all three showings, third was comped as per notes. That'll be $250,000."

Carson let out a cough. *A quarter mill?*

"Are you shitting me?"

"No, sir. That's standard. I gave you the first viewing rate as well."

"Wow. OK. I'll be right back."

Before the man could reply, Carson pushed through the door and walked quickly away. He saw several men in business suits approaching the entrance.

"Guess that soldier couldn't stomach the show," one said, getting a laugh from the group.

Carson turned, the look on his face enough to shut them up.

He went through the next door, finding himself in yet another lobby. This one was a traditional hotel lobby. He suspected those men must fly in and stay on site, filling their time by paying for depravity.

Carson crossed the second lobby, doing his best to not make any eye contact. To his right was the check-in area, half a dozen people milling around while the employee sorted their rooms. To his left was a bank of windows, which looked out over the tarmac. A number of airplanes were lined up. Some were military, while others were private jets. He spotted motion and stopped to look. A group of soldiers were approaching the complex, a practiced formation in action.

That's not good, he thought. If someone spotted him, he'd be called over, expected to join the ranks. Or worse, discovered.

It didn't matter either way.

As he arrived at the main door, an alarm began to blare.

"BREACH! BREACH! BREACH!"

Carson didn't know if it was himself who'd been discovered or Tyler, but he didn't care. All he knew was that he needed to find Tyler and they needed to escape.

36

Tyler had just made it back to where they'd agreed to meet when the alarm went off.

He figured Dr. Meddle must have got free and triggered it, unless Carson had been discovered. He knew someone would come inspect this level shortly, so he tried the only door that was solid wood along the way, breathing a sigh of relief when it opened.

Janitor's closet.

Of course.

Tyler pulled the janitor's cart out and angled it so that it hid him in the doorway, but still allowed him to see down the hall in either direction. He kept touching the photo in his pocket, kept thinking about what had become of his parents. Why did this need to happen? *Why them? Why him?*

The door to the stairwell burst open and before Tyler could see who it was, the soldier was almost on top of him. He tried to push the cart into the person's body, but they sidestepped his attempt and grabbed him around his arm.

"Tyler, we need to get moving," Carson said, pulling him

towards the stairwell. He'd never been more relieved that it'd been Carson.

They took the stairs down two and even three at a time. All the while the hideous voice boomed throughout the complex, already driving them crazy.

"BREACH! BREACH! BREACH!"

Footsteps from above echoed throughout the confirmed space.

When they arrived at the ground level, they kicked the door open and rushed out, not caring that a firing squad might've been waiting for them.

Carson took an immediate right, keeping tight to the outer wall of the building. They shuffled along, using the bushes as concealment. They paused and crouched lower as soldiers scurried by, then carried on when the coast was clear. Arriving at the back corner, they found they were near the guard tower that'd been their way in. Only this time they could see two guards watching from the windows.

"Shit, someone's in there," Carson said.

They kneeled, catching their breath, both running scenarios through their heads.

"What now? Any ideas?" Tyler asked. He looked at the fence knowing there was no way to climb over or dig under. They didn't have tools to cut through. Their only option was to somehow get into that guard tower and climb down, but that would expose them.

"We could figure out a decoy or distraction. Jesus, just saying that sounds stupid. I'm honestly stumped, Tyler."

A noise to their left got their attention. Two soldiers were holding onto thick chains, visibly straining against whatever was attached to the other end.

They yanked on the chains, and the creature changed direction and came around the side of the building.

They'd both seen their fair share of horrific things in this basin and in the complex, but it was always a shock when a new experiment came into view.

The chains led from the soldiers to the neck of a hideous beast that was part man, part rhino and part bull. It's massive, barrel chest led to a thick neck and impressive horns on either side of its wide face.

From their hiding spot, Tyler could see large gashes that ran all over the beast's body, and as it lumbered forward, blood and bits of tissue pumped out with each step.

"Release C-11223," a voice commanded.

The two soldiers dropped the chains and the creature burst forward, dropping to all fours and barreling directly towards them with a roar.

"We gotta move!" Carson yelled as he sprinted to the ladder. Tyler didn't think it was their best option, but followed, not knowing what else to do. If he stayed, he'd surely be gored to death.

Carson was almost halfway up by the time Tyler made it to the bottom and started climbing. He was shocked at the speed with which Carson was moving. Behind him, the creature closed the distance and Tyler knew he needed to be at least ten feet up to prevent it from being able to grab him, if not more.

A noise from above made him look up, and he saw the hatch door was open, and Carson and a guard were grappling, arms entwined.

Tyler kept climbing, not sure what to do. He was essentially trapped and as he saw it, an open target for anyone with a gun.

As if waiting for him to think that, he looked to see where the beast was, but instead found three soldiers approaching the tower, guns held against their shoulders.

The beast below lowered its rhino-horned head and began to ram into the base. With each blow the ladder shook, the guard shack vibrating.

"Hold steady!" a soldier directed with a shout. Tyler watched as someone walked over and stopped beside the soldiers. "Guns down," he said, touching the nearest soldier on their arm. In unison, the three lowered their guns, but kept them at a ready position. The man wore a suit, which seemed strange to Tyler. Wouldn't they be in fatigues like the rest? He looked very familiar, Tyler struggling to place where he'd seen the man before.

The beast slammed into the bottom of the ladder once again, but this worked in Carson's favor. The guard stumbled and Carson pulled hard with one hand, while grabbing the ladder tight with the other. Tyler saw what was happening just in time and leaned as far to his right as he could. The guard pitched forward and fell to the ground, just missing colliding with Tyler. The guard landed head-first, the sound of his neck snapping making Tyler gag in disgust.

The second guard was now grabbing Carson, but for whatever reason, they weren't thinking their strategy through. Instead of keeping Carson where he was or trying to throw him to the ground, he hoisted Carson into the guard tower. Tyler saw his chance to get inside.

He scrambled.

"Fire!"

The man in the suit gave the command just as Tyler pulled his legs into the guard tower. The guns cracked, the bullets zinging and ricocheting off the bottom of the tower. Tyler slammed the hatch down, then stood to see how Carson was doing.

The soldier and the officer were locked together, looking

like two wrestlers trying to gain an advantage. Carson was taller than the soldier by at least four inches, but the soldier looked to have fifty pounds on Carson. Combined, it meant that the two were pushing against each other with neither gaining the upper hand.

Tyler moved around behind the soldier and took a running start before leaping and landing a drop kick square in their back. It sent both the soldier and Carson tumbling and, in the melee, the soldier ended up on top of Carson directly beside the hatch. This time the man popped the hatch open and shoved Carson over the opening. The beast below was still slamming and bashing the ladder. The three soldiers and the man in the suit appeared below as well, the three guns all trained on Carson.

Tyler rushed to help but stopped when a familiar bellow came from the trees. Looking over, he saw the trees bend and sway as something immense moved to the fence. Long horns rattled and clanked against the trees as the beast approached the guard tower.

Another bellow erupted and the windows shook.

Below, the soldiers were pointing their guns at the beast beyond the fence and back to Carson and then back to the beast.

The man in the suit's eyes were wide, seeing this creature so close.

"Tyler..." Carson managed, as the guard continued to force him through the opening. "Tyler... go," Carson said, one last time. Then he reached up, grabbed the guard in a bear hug and before Tyler could react, the two of them fell through the opening.

37

———

Tyler was shocked at what'd just happened.

Carson and the guard disappeared from sight.

The animal bellowed louder, more aggressively, forcing Tyler to turn. An impossibly thick horn sped towards the windows before shattering them with an impact that caused the top of the tower to shudder and sway.

From below, he heard the hard thud as Carson and the guard landed on the ground. The soldiers below shouted orders to not move, to stay still. Tyler heard someone ask if they were alive.

The man in the suit shouted over the commotion, commanding someone to get in the tower. It was then that it clicked. *Mr. Adams.* The owner of the mining company. His dad's boss. It all made sense now as to why they wanted Tyler to sign that compensation contract and to move on.

"Get a tracker on that beast," someone else yelled.

The sound of boots hitting the ladder snapped Tyler out of his stupor.

He rushed to the far side, then, saying a silent prayer, sprinted forward.

He didn't know how far away the animal was, or if he'd even clear the fence, but he had to put his trust in this mysterious beast that continued to be there for him.

As Tyler jumped through the jagged opening, he saw the animal push the fence down with one enormous hand. His trajectory was lower than he'd hoped, which caused him to slam into the ribs of the beast, bouncing off and landing with enough force to knock the wind out of him. His head struck something solid on the ground, rattling his vision. As he struggled to stand, he felt the beast wrap a massive hand around his midsection and hoist him onto its back. Then they were off, careening into the forest, leaving the shouts and the soldiers and the complex behind them.

Tyler lost sight of the buildings as his eyes slipped shut and unconsciousness took hold.

38

———————

HOW LONG WAS HE OUT FOR?

He wasn't sure. Tyler remembered hard bumps and jostles that almost sent him flying off the shoulders of his guardian, but he somehow managed to remain in place. Or, more likely, this creature made sure he didn't fall off. Even when it was sprinting through the woods at an ungodly speed, it made sure Tyler never fell.

While things flashed and fluttered before his eyes as he fought to stay conscious, he was positive he saw the large wall at some point, but that may just have been his brain recalling his journey, filling in the blank spaces.

The weather changed the further they travelled from the complex, going from a clear, sunny day to overcast and then the beginning of rain.

He tried to use the animal as protection, but it was no use. Soon he was soaked through and began to shiver.

As thunder rumbled, the beast turned towards an area that had once been leveled by a slide along the wall of the valley. Ahead was a dark opening. Entering, it softly set the human on the ground. The animal delicately eased itself to the dirt, positioning itself around the man. It pulled the figure closer into its body, trying its best to warm the man and keep him dry.

Outside the rain fell and the storm increased in intensity.

39

Birds chirped and a woodpecker rattled against a tree.

Something nearby scurried away as Tyler stirred.

It was only the pounding in his head that reminded him that this wasn't a camping trip.

He was alone now; his guardian having moved on at some point earlier. His clothes were still damp, but he didn't wake cold. He suspected his friend hadn't left that long ago.

Sitting, Tyler waited until the throb behind his eyes settled. When he placed his hands against them to try and help, his palms felt something sticky. Looking at them, he found the familiar redness of blood.

He knew he'd hit his head hard, but how much damage had he done?

When he finally believed it was safe to do so, he stood. Thankfully nothing spun and he didn't feel as though he was going to vomit or pass out. The first few steps were tentative at best, but his legs were solid, and the ground wasn't jelly. He walked to the opening of the cave they'd hunkered down in. From where he stood, he could see the complex far off in the distance as well as the green wall that blocked the way. A small plane was coming in from further beyond it, but Tyler was too far away to see it land.

Taking a step out of the cave, the sun shone down, helping to warm him.

He started to smile at the feeling of the rays on his face when everything came back. *Carson.*

It was just him.

Carson was most likely dead. If not, he was in the process of being experimented on. Tortured to be transformed. Mr. Adams, mister man in the suit, would've already sent soldiers in pursuit of Tyler. His parents were no longer his parents. Already sliced and diced, reduced to monstrosities and medical numbers.

There was only one option for Tyler now.

His only option was to flee and make it back to civilization as fast as he could. He knew he wouldn't be safe, even once he crossed that perimeter marker, but if he could just get to the SUV and drive into town then maybe, just maybe, he could survive. They were already after him. He knew that. Tyler figured they'd be after him for the rest of his life. But he wasn't about to just give up. Not after all of this.

Examining his location in the valley, Tyler was happy that his guardian had transported him in the right direction. It would still be a day's hike to get back to the perimeter. That was, if his head allowed it. He knew an injury like this was no joke, but he'd have to push it, force himself beyond the pain.

Knowing he had a long day ahead, he reached for his bag ready to leave. When his hand found nothing, he was confused. He'd had it at the complex. Did he leave it? Had it been on his back when he jumped from the tower? It was fuzzy trying to put the details together. He was pretty sure that Carson had suggested they leave their bags where they found the fatigues. He was still wearing the soldiers gear they'd found. The left side of his jacket had dried blood down the front, and one leg had some small cuts in it, most likely from broken glass. But no recollection of what'd happened with his bag.

Something niggled at him about this. There was a reason not having his bag was a big deal, but he couldn't fully form the thoughts. Sure, it was a great inconvenience not having any of the food packs or his water pouch available, but he could make do. But there was something else that was missing from the equation.

He resigned himself to just put it aside for the time being. *Bigger fish to fry*, his dad would've said.

He double checked the cave one last time before departing. Finding nothing of use, he set out towards where he'd entered the area all those days ago.

40

WAS IT THE BLOW TO THE HEAD OR THE LEVEL OF EXHAUSTION he'd reached that made his legs feel like concrete?

He'd been walking through the trees for a solid hour, but already he was wiped and he had a nagging suspicion that he'd barely covered any distance.

Tyler had to stop and lean against a rock, reaching absently for his water pouch. But he had nothing. His pack. God, how he missed it right now. A familiar weight was missing, not only robbing him of water but also creating a feeling of being exposed without it nestled comfortably on his back.

He licked his lips, letting his saliva act as a lubricant. His tongue was heavy. Dehydration was coming.

"Hey, good morning. I didn't even see you sitting there."

An old man spoke to him at such a close distance that Tyler screamed and stumbled, falling to the ground. The impact jarred his head, his teeth slamming shut with a painful clack.

"Oh, my! I'm so sorry to have frightened you," the man said, shuffling closer.

Tyler had to blink a few times before his vision cleared. He wasn't imagining this. It wasn't a hallucination. Even after all he'd been through, and several blows to his head, this was real.

A short, rotund man of about sixty stood a few feet away, leaning over in concern. He sported a grey beard that extended down to his waist. His head was bald which really looked strange when compared to the grand beard he had grown. It was only when Tyler took in the man's features that he could see something was off.

"Are you an experiment?"

The bluntness of his question made Tyler cringe. He hadn't meant to sound so offensive.

"Ach. Yeah, 'fraid so," he said with a wave of his hand, as though he was used to having random people in the woods question how he'd come to exist in his current state.

The man's dirt-covered, faded trench coat didn't fit him well. Whatever was underneath was most likely something Tyler didn't want to see.

"Did Mr. Adams send you to kill me?"

The man barked out a laugh that turned into a coughing fit. He doubled over, holding his protruding stomach as he hacked up phlegm. Spitting it off into the distance, he wiped his lips, examining the thick substance before he returned his attention to Tyler.

"Not that I know of. *Should* I kill you?"

"I'd appreciate it if you didn't," Tyler replied, smiling at the man.

The man stepped forward and extended a hand. Tyler took it and thanked him as he got back to his feet. His head swam and his legs felt like jelly, but he managed to steady himself.

"Name's Tyler."

"Pleased to meet you Tyler. I'm B-88899."

"B-88899? Do you not have a *human* name? Or don't you remember your real name?"

"Nah. They scramble everything pretty good. Or so I hear. I broke out a few years back. Just been keeping low and hiding as best I can. Although whenever I hear that beeping at night, I pray that I'll wake up in the morning."

Tyler nodded. He was surprised that this man had made himself known to him. After all, Tyler was still wearing the uniform.

"Why'd you come speak to me?"

"I recognized you from the other day when you snuck in. I was at the edge of the perimeter collecting blackberries. Saw a young lad figure out the cameras and the guards. Came hustling into no-man's land. In fact, I think you almost spotted me. When I saw you leaning there just now, I thought '*B-88899, that boy's a nice-looking chap. Let's go say hello.'* So I did."

Everything about the man, his mannerisms and the interaction, made Tyler smile. But it also set alarm bells ringing. He no longer had someone else to bounce things off, no Carson to use his "cop-gut" about a situation. He would keep his guard up as best he could around him.

"B-88899, do you have a water source, nearby? I'm very thirsty and misplaced my pack."

"Absolutely. Come, my boy. Let's drink and take shelter from this sun. It's a hot one today."

Tyler watched the man walk, which was a sight to behold. It looked like he may have more than two legs, mostly because of the odd bulge around his midsection. The jacket was doing a good job of keeping whatever was happening beneath it hidden.

He thought back to when he'd first entered the perimeter. He remembered the feeling that someone was nearby, but hadn't thought of it since. B-88899 sounded sincere enough when he said he'd watched Tyler infiltrate the woods, but Tyler was exhausted by all of the oddities and strangeness he'd encountered. He wasn't sure what to believe anymore.

"My boy, what a wondrous day. I can't believe my good fortune. To run into a lad such as yourself. My, what a good day, yes."

Tyler slowed as they walked, letting more space grow between them. The man was talking to himself in a way that set off every *'run'* alarm in his head. Was he hallucinating this figure who talked as though he was an actor in a fantasy movie? He didn't believe so, but this could be the signs of a serious head injury.

The path they were following weaved through the trees, but it was still heading in the direction he needed to travel. Something still nagged at him, about that entire scenario and his missing bag, but the fogginess still had a grasp on what exactly.

Maybe I'm still sleeping? Maybe this is a dream?

No sooner had he thought that, then he kicked an unseen root, pain shooting up his foot and his head screaming from the impact. He was definitely awake.

Ahead of them, a clearing was beginning to emerge through the trees, Tyler already able to see the shimmer and reflection of the sun off the water.

"Here we go, my boy. Water. Fresh, delicious water. Have your fill."

Tyler stepped past the man, thankful for the wonderful sight. He made his way to the water's edge, then stooped. Cupping his hands, he brought the cold liquid to his mouth and savored the crispness as he sloshed it around.

"That's delicious," he said, turning to see what the man was doing.

He found him leaning under a tree, fast asleep. His light snores caused each exhale to jiggle his cheeks.

Turning back to take another drink, he didn't see the man peek at him, his attention focused on filling his cupped hands.

41

———

AN ELECTRIC SHOCK PULSED THROUGH HIM, BRINGING FORTH A scream and his body jolted and shuddered.

Carson's eyes shot open.

He was on the ground, staring up at the guard tower.

It took a second but it came back. He'd pulled the soldier with him through the opening, hopefully letting Tyler escape.

A ringing in his ears prevented him from hearing anything other than the high pitched noise that ricocheted around his head, but he could see scrambled movement in his peripheral vision. He tried to roll onto his side but couldn't. He realized he had no sensation in his legs at all.

Forcing his neck to bend as much as he could, he looked down to see what the hell was going on with his legs.

His left leg was twisted at an unnatural angle towards him, as though it had been attached backwards and he was trying to kick his own stomach. His guts lurched at the visual, his brain processing a tiny amount of that data. When he looked over at his right leg, he puked. He couldn't roll over, so it just pulsed up in a wave before slopping back between his lips. He started to choke, coughing and sputtering. He panicked, the reality that he was going to asphyxiate on his own vomit making his eyes bulge. A nearby soldier heard the commotion and came over.

"Hey, he's choking, give me a hand."

A soldier stepped beside Carson and started to bend down to roll him over when Mr. Adams grabbed the soldier's arm.

"Leave him. I need that trace on that beast and I need it now," Mr. Adams said.

Carson continued choking, trying to force the vomit out, but it wouldn't leave his mouth, wouldn't eject from his throat. While he couldn't feel anything below his waist, his lungs screamed with agony and his chest felt like it was being stabbed with each attempt to take in air but also clear his mouth and throat with coughs.

It was no use. He faded. His vision blurred, his body spasmed. He still had the droning ringing in his ears but that grew softer and softer, as things shut down.

The last thing he thought before everything went black was where his missing right leg was.

42

———

Laboratory lights blurred by the liquid layer of being in an incubation chamber were what greeted Carson as he returned to the land of the living once again.

Only this time, he had no recollection of the life he'd lived before.

Gone were his name, job, memories and identity.

In its place was K-00001.

The first of the new group, the first of *this* particular attempt at hybridization.

Moving his arms and legs, his brain struggled to process the visual of the praying mantis limbs.

That's not right, he thought, but he didn't know *why* it wasn't right.

His forelegs darted out and in, seemingly trying to catch debris as it floated by.

Remaining still, he caught a reflection of himself in the curve of the tube. He still had some of his human face, mainly his eyes, but otherwise his head was enlarged, and his eyes bulged to the sides.

"Aaaahhhhhhhhhhhhhh," he screamed, immediately

sucking in a mouthful of fluid. He coughed and sputtered again, but it didn't matter. He was enclosed in a tube of fluid. This action – of choking – almost brought another memory to the surface, but once again, it floated away before becoming visible, taken with the tide of amnesia.

A few men in lab coats were moving around which he found far more enthralling than he should have, but it was a woman who left the group and walked over to his enclosure, pushing something, that really got his attention. The latch of the tube opened and the fluid splashed out. Once this happened, Carson was able to let out a solid cough.

"Thank you," he said, stepping forward on his strange, skinny legs.

"End it," she said, turning and walking away.

The click of a gun cocking brought back another memory locked in the vault. His head twisted, visions of a patrol car and lights flashing.

The trigger was pulled, ending any chance of that memory becoming meaningful and in moments a cleaning crew moved in to mop up the remains of K-00001.

43

Tyler let B-88899 sleep for another hour. He knew he should be making his way back to the perimeter, but it was just too nice here and his body told him he needed this break.

He sat near the water, listening to the bird calls, letting the breeze blow over him.

His head had returned to some semblance of normality. When he turned or looked down, he didn't see any spots or feel dizzy, and standing didn't bring on any vertigo. He thought, if he needed to, he'd be able to run, but for how long or how fast he didn't know. But survival was priority number one. He'd push it to the limit if necessary.

"I need to get going," he said to the snoozing man. Once again he reached absently for a pack that wasn't there. His hand opened and closed a few times, fingers dancing to connect with something resembling cloth. Finding none, he looked at the place he believed his bag would be with some confusion, then remembered that it was back in the complex. It was probably being sifted through and inventoried by the soldiers at this very moment

He left the man sleeping at the base of the tree, making his way around the edge of the water. He could see, far off ahead, the exact place he needed to get to. Once there, it would be a steep climb, then across the forest to the perimeter. It was funny that he remembered it so well, especially with everything that had happened between then and now.

The ground along the water's edge was mushy, but he was almost to the trees. Once he got to the forest line he turned to look back once more at the sleeping man when B-88899 spoke.

"Might I walk with you a bit, lad? I'm so awfully lonely."

He should've jumped or screamed, but instead he gave a nod, not wanting to be rude. He hadn't even heard B-88899 moving. No part of him wanted this strange man to travel with him, but he was worried what would happen if he said no and he grew angry.

He picked up the pace, to a speed he himself wasn't all that comfortable with, but he hoped it would be enough to have the man decide to stay behind.

"Head doing better?" he asked, as Tyler grew the gap between them some more.

"A bit, I just need to get out of here before they find me," he replied, over his shoulder.

A strange sound started from behind. A scurrying sound. It reminded Tyler of an insect scuttling across a metallic surface.

It was that image that made Tyler turn.

B-88899 had removed his pants. Tyler had been right. The man moved forward on six legs, giving Tyler the impression that the man was riding a beetle.

"You forced me to do this," he said matter-of-factly. "To keep up with you, I couldn't keep pretending."

Tyler began walking again, getting as close to a jog as he

could. He was worried about how his body would respond if he broke into a run.

"Boy, you better stop running. I need to eat, and *they* need your corpse," B-88899 yelled, all illusions of camaraderie tossed aside.

The man's tone of voice had turned predatory. That was all it took for Tyler to shift into the next gear.

He took off running, focusing on keeping his head steady and his breathing manageable. It was a fraction easier not having a backpack that jostled and rattled around behind him, but that was minor compared to how gross he was starting to feel with each deep inhale and exhale. The ground was flat enough that he didn't feel his brain rattling around as he went, and he was glad to see that his legs were allowing this level of exertion.

B-88899 shouted again from behind him, but Tyler had moved far enough ahead that he couldn't make out the words. He glanced back, finding he'd lost sight of the man.

That's when what needed to happen occurred. It would've been something Carson suggested, but now it came to Tyler. He skidded to a stop and stepped off the trail. He found a rock that had good weight in his hand. Tyler hid until the man scuttled by, still in hot pursuit. As he went by, Tyler jumped out and brought the rock down as hard as he could on top of his head. B-88899 crumpled to the ground from the blow. His insectile legs kicked and spasmed as he grunted and gurgled. Tyler continued to rain down blow upon blow to the man's head until there was no more movement, no more sounds.

It was only after he tossed the rock away that he spotted something sticking out from the inside pocket of the man's jacket. He delicately reached in, retrieved it and pulled it out.

He was looking at his own yearbook photo.

On the back were his name and age written in pen.

B-88899 had been sent after him.

Instinctively, Tyler searched the immediate surrounding area. Seeing nothing that worried him, he used the man's coat to pull him off the trail, then covered his remains crudely with branches. He hoped wildlife would get rid of the carcass before someone found it.

He left B-88899 behind. He should've trusted his gut more, but he chalked that up to his head injury.

Or loneliness.

The sun had travelled further across the sky than he liked, so he decided to jog as much as his body would allow. He needed to get as close to the perimeter as he could, knowing he'd be spending another night in this place.

44

———————

HIS BODY TOLD HIM THIS WAS ALL IT HAD. HE WAS EXHAUSTED, thirsty, and his headache had come back full force. He needed to stop. He'd run through the forest, trying his best to ignore anything and everything behind him, but he could no longer keep going, not at this pace.

Slumping against the base of a tree, Tyler found some shade. Realizing he was still sitting along the animal trail he'd been following, he forced his aching body to crawl around to the backside of the tree. Now he was at least out of view from anyone that might be by, and knowing there was a high chance he'd slip into a nap this at least offered him the illusion of safety.

No sooner had he worked his body into some semblance of a comfortable position than his eyes grew heavy, his breathing slowed, and he started to fight sleep. Too many things out there wanted to devour him, or even worse, find him and slice and dice his body. His head bobbed as he struggled to remain awake.

The approach of a vehicle sounded nearby. Even with how tired he was, that blasted him wide awake with a surge of adrenalin. He rushed through the forest in the direction the noise was coming from, much to his legs' dismay.

Was there a road here?

He had such a one-track mind, totally focused on getting out of this basin that he hadn't even thought about the map he'd seen or the one Carson had. Of course there was a road near here.

Tyler approached the ridge, catching movement through the trees. Soldiers were milling around a Jeep. He'd seen so many of them now that even the camouflage on their fatigues and the paint scheme didn't disguise them anymore. Someone stepped out of the Jeep, went to the back, and grabbed something that was blocked from his view from where he crouched.

The man tossed it onto the ground and stepped back.

"You there," he said, pointing to a soldier standing close. "Four shots. Adams wants us to be absolutely certain."

The soldier stepped forward, pointed his sidearm, and popped off four shots.

"Return to base," the man said, hopping back into the Jeep and driving away as the soldiers piled into the back of a large truck before it followed.

Tyler knew to wait. Whether this was a trap, something strategically done to draw him from cover or not, he was taking no chances.

So, he patiently waited.

The sun worked its way across the sky, the temperature inching higher and higher. Tyler was thankful that where he'd hunkered down was shielded, but it didn't stop his growing hunger or thirst. He was sweating far more than he'd like, especially knowing that he had nothing to replenish the water loss with.

His mind started to wander.

Loneliness and isolation have a way of catching up on someone. Couple that with hunger, exhaustion and a head injury and before he knew it, Tyler was standing, trying to see just what the group had dumped.

It was during this moment, stretching as tall as he could, that he saw it sitting beside the lump.

A canteen.

It couldn't be? Could it?

It was a trap. Tyler knew it, his mouth knew it, his legs knew it.

But still...

He took a step forward but paused when a raccoon came waddling out from a bush. It walked directly to the canteen. It stopped, gave it a once over, its nose wiggling furiously as it took in the foreign smells before it. Feeling comfortable, it reached out and grasped the canteen in its human-like hands.

There was an immediate reaction.

The raccoon began to squeal and froth, foam bubbling from its mouth. It twitched and convulsed, before it rolled onto its back. It was trying to get away from the canteen, but when the animal fell the canteen landed on the animal's stomach and burned into the mammal.

Tyler watched in shock as the poor animal writhed in pain. The canteen must have been covered in something extremely corrosive, because in only a short amount of time, it slid through the midsection of the raccoon. Somehow, the animal remained alive. It pulled its front half a short distance away, a gaping hole through its body. It screamed the entire time, enough to make Tyler cover his ears. Finally, the animal let out its last moan and collapsed, no longer moving.

The canteen had been a trap, Tyler thought. The soldiers

had left it for him. They suspected he'd come this way. Or maybe they were thinking B-88899 would lead him here.

Either way, they'd expected Tyler to rush from where he was hiding, grab the canteen, and be brutally burned. Whatever coated the canteen interested Tyler, purely because it had vaporized the animal while the canteen itself remained unscathed.

He sat back down, staring at the object. His curiosity wanted him to look so badly, but after seeing what had happened to that poor raccoon, he was even more hesitant.

He didn't know why, but he remained sitting. Ideally, he should be covering more ground, getting closer and closer to the perimeter with every passing minute. But something told him to be patient.

Part of him expected to hear a familiar bellow from his guardian at any moment.

Something moved in the trees from the opposite side of the clearing. It took a few minutes before they came into view. Tyler watched as a coyote trotted over to the object that the soldier had left, completely ignoring the canteen. It sniffed it twice before sniffing the raccoon. Its face contorted when it inhaled the raccoon's scent, returning to the object. It tentatively reached in with its snout and snagged something with its teeth. It pulled and wiggled and started to extract whatever it was that was within.

Tyler jumped up in excitement, wanting to see what it was but his sudden movement startled the coyote and it darted away.

He decided it was now or never. He'd see what they'd left behind and continue to the perimeter.

Making his way to the object, he made sure to give the canteen a wide berth. The object had an unusual shape, a black garbage bag concealing whatever was inside. The coyote had ripped some of the bag open but whatever was inside was still obscured from him. Using his foot, Tyler pushed the bag back only to let out a shout.

Inside the bag was the remains of an immense insect.

Tyler crouched to get a closer look, when he saw it. Half its face. Human. *Carson.*

He turned and spewed stomach bile and water over the clearing beside him.

His friend. *Transformed. Murdered.*

He retched again, which brought on a series of dry heaves, his stomach cramping and clenching painfully.

Returning to the bag, he kneeled and looked at the soulless eyes that stared back. In a war movie, the soldier would reach out, pluck the dog tags off and stow them in their pocket for safekeeping and delivery to a loved one in the future. Not in this movie, not in this clearing.

Instead, Tyler pulled the tattered garbage bag back over the human-insect's head, doing his best to cover Carson.

He couldn't leave him like this. Either of them. He went to the trees, grabbed some branches and returned. Laying them over the body of the raccoon, he wanted to give the little animal a sendoff as well, but saw that its fur was still matted with the corrosive material. The branches began to crackle and dissolve as soon as contact was made.

So, he left them both there, as they were. Unfortunately, some animal would come along and try to snack on the raccoon, not knowing their mistake until it was too late. Maybe all the forest creatures would smell something wrong with the carcass and leave it be?

But Tyler knew that Carson's remains wouldn't be so lucky.

45

A light rain started soon after Tyler crested a hill and left Carson's body behind for good.

He was mentally done. A broken man. Cold, wet, hungry, thirsty, exhausted and in pain, he wanted nothing more than to just sit down and die.

What was there left to return to?

His grandfather.

That was who was left and who he needed to focus on and use as motivation to not give up.

His grandmother had passed away a few years back and while his grandfather was fairly active for a man his age, Tyler knew that if he lost his grandson as well as his son, he'd also give up. His world would be shattered.

Nope, Tyler wasn't going to let that happen.

Not today.

He took a breath, focused on his surroundings, and continued.

Tyler kept looking for anything he could ingest or drink. Surely, with the rain falling, some water would collect somewhere.

In the distance, thunder rumbled. Tyler watched the clouds forming, growing darker. They were moving towards his location, which meant heavier rain and wind would arrive shortly. He switched his focus to finding shelter. Staying out of a storm was more important than getting drenched for some food or water. He'd keep looking for either, but he didn't want to freeze to death. He figured he'd make it to the perimeter by tomorrow afternoon. That was, as long as nothing else brought his journey to a standstill.

A few hundred yards ahead, Tyler spotted an odd shape in the trees. He stopped and stepped behind a thick tree close to him. Watching it, he saw no movement, no change in shape. *Was it a structure? It couldn't be, could it?*

From somewhere nearby, the familiar bellow erupted. That was all he needed to hear. He jogged towards it, his legs angry with the exertion.

It was a monitoring shack.

From the outside it was almost an exact replica of the one Carson had brought him to. For a brief moment, Tyler worried that he'd somehow looped back around in the wrong direction. But only for a moment. He climbed the ladder, pushed the hatch open and pulled himself through.

What he found surprised him.

This was an *active* monitoring shack.

Monitors showed video feeds from cameras placed throughout the woods. He found notes jotted down on pads of paper as well as an open document where whoever had been here had been typing up things spotted on the screens. There was even one that was displaying a message;

"Complex breach. Monitoring stations to report directly to main bunker."

That explained why it was unmanned. Tyler hadn't even thought about the potential of entering the structure only to meet a soldier or multiple soldiers. A bit of luck that was most appreciated.

Taking stock of what was here, he saw the usual screens and maps. He saw the fireplace had burned down to coals, but jabbing at it with the poker, red and orange peeked through. Tyler grabbed some wood from a small pile beside the fireplace and set them on the embers.

So, it hadn't been long since they left.

As the flames crackled and grew, so did the warmth. Tyler was no longer shivering. He took off the jacket and shirt and laid it near the fire, letting it dry. He did the same with his boots, socks and pants, leaving just his boxers on.

The fire was now roaring and with that came light in the corners of the room. Tyler could've cried. On one side of the station was a shelf filled with canned food and bottles of water. He even saw some juice boxes. Whoever manned this station must have grown tired of what was supplied to them and stocked this on their own.

He grabbed a half dozen juice boxes and two bottles of water, setting them on the floor by his clothes. Next he grabbed a box of cookies as well as two cans of beans. They had pop-top lids, so he pulled the tab and freed the brown syrup and beans. Finding a camping pot, he poured the two cans in and set it by the flames, letting the fire warm the contents while he inhaled the cookies and greedily slurped the juice.

Once the six juices were done, he went and grabbed six more. He plopped himself down in a chair in front of the monitors, watching the screens, feeling like an unseen King surveying his lands.

At first nothing moved. He kept looking from one screen to the next, hoping to see something, anything. After going through each of the three screens a few times he noticed a flashing red dot on the fourth screen. Moving the mouse, the fourth screen came to life. Tyler discovered the feed matrix. The screen was segmented into twelve small squares with the middle square flashing. He clicked on it and the middle monitor of the main computers changed to show the view he'd clicked.

It was where he'd left Carson's body.

The back half of a Jeep was visible. Two soldiers were standing there, assault rifles at the ready. They scanned the area as though something was nearby. Another soldier was in the process of burying the raccoon's remains. Tyler didn't give him much notice. Instead, he focused on the fire that was burning beside it. He watched as Carson's remains popped and sizzled and even though there was no sound, the fire that was burning behind him in the station created the soundtrack for him in eerie synchronicity.

Tyler had to pry his eyes from the screen, but he felt much better not watching his dead friend burn. As much as he was curious about the soldiers, some things were best not watched. He pulled the beans from where they had heated up. He reflected while eating them, thinking back to all of the camping trips he'd taken with his father where one of them had inevitably scorched the roof of their mouth or burned their tongues by being too eager to eat food heated by a fire. Beans had always been a food staple on these trips, the taste alone transporting him back to hundreds of shared evenings under the stars.

Neil.

Sandra.

Both gone but both still here.

Tyler tried to wrap his head around that sentiment. As

far as he was concerned, his parents were dead. He didn't care anymore if they were a living entity, they were no longer human, no longer *them*. He wondered if his father had already been deployed to some far-off region, tasked to act as some super soldier for this secret corporation.

Would they have proper funerals for them once he was back?

That thought finally broke him and his beans began to be dampened by the falling tears. Tyler had never cried for his mother. Not like this. She'd never been a real, tangible thing for him. She'd always just been photographs and stories.

Now, he'd come so close to physical reconnection. To actually meeting his mom, even though she was a file number and a fucked-up science experiment.

His heart wished they'd met. His brain was happy they hadn't.

Finishing the beans, he knew he needed to sleep, but the thought of closing his eyes brought fear. What if a soldier returned while he was sleeping?

He pulled some heavier boxes and a chair over and slid them on the latch. He made sure the sliding lock was in place. He hoped that would be enough to prevent anyone from entering, but at the very least it would alert him to someone trying to get in. He got dressed, knowing that if someone did surprise him, he'd not want to be caught in just his boxers.

The floor of the shack should've been rock hard, but once he found a decently comfortable position on his back, his exhaustion took over.

Sleep came fast and hard.

As he drifted off to sleep, there was motion on the screen. The soldiers got in the Jeep, which backed up and pulled around so that it was facing directly at the camera Tyler had been watching.

The driver pointed and mouthed something before the soldier in the passenger seat took aim and fired.

The monitor showed only static.

Tyler was already snoring.

46

———

The rumble of an engine.

He'd been dreaming of sitting on a sandy beach while his parents sat beside him. Tyler knew he'd been happy in that dream. Full of love. But it was the rumble of an engine that caused him to look down the length of the beach, and finding a military Jeep approaching, Tyler realized this wasn't part of the dream.

The shouts of soldiers and the noise of them moving under the monitoring station got his full attention.

Tyler went to stand before thinking someone may be watching through the windows, so he remained crouched.

A thud sounded.

He looked over, watched as another thud happened and the chair and box he'd placed on the latch jumped from the impact from below.

"Locked, sir. Feels like something's on top of it."

"If the latch won't budge, open fire. We want him alive, but maybe a few wounds will make him think twice," a voice replied which Tyler recognized immediately as Mr. Adams.

They were going to shoot through the floor.

It was wood, which wasn't going to act as much of a barrier at all. Tyler scanned the room, looking for anything of use. The fire had burned out, so he rushed over, standing as close as possible. They'd most likely shoot towards the middle of the room. Logic suggested it was safest to stay at the edge of the shack.

He heard the click of the weapons as they readied, followed by a loud explosive boom as several soldiers squeezed the triggers on their assault rifles. The floor had small spots explode up all over as the wood splintered and flew into the air. This went on for a full thirty seconds, the soldiers seemingly walking around the base of the station in a circle. As the bullets peppered the floor directly before Tyler, he squeezed as close to the wall as he could, face turned away. He thought for sure there would be no surviving this, but as the soldiers continued moving, the bullets followed, and he found that when everything went silent he'd not even been grazed.

"See any blood?" a voice asked, coming from directly below where Tyler stood. Tyler dared not move, lest he alerted them to his position.

"Negative."

"Again," Mr. Adams commanded.

Tyler braced himself again, hugging the wall as tightly as he could.

The rifles erupted, the soldiers repeating their circle.

"Cease fire," someone else commanded.

The gunfire went silent.

"Pack up. Let's go boys, in the Jeeps. We got a report of imminent approach. Double time."

Tyler had no idea what that meant, but even from here he heard rushed movement and the sounds of the soldiers piling into the Jeeps. The engines returned to life, followed by the vehicles speeding off leaving Tyler in dead silence.

Another trap?

He didn't understand. Why would they be so hell-bent on getting him out of this station to just pack up and leave? What did imminent approach mean?

As if it had been waiting to answer, a roar erupted throughout the forest. Whatever made that noise was massive.

Imminent approach.

He understood now. Tyler rushed to the windows, searching for the creature. A second roar rattled the windows, and as Tyler stared out of the glass, he saw the trees begin to sway and move. Whatever this enormous beast was, it was easily pushing through the forest. It was bigger than the lizard creature he and Carson had encountered at the wall. Tyler suspected it was even larger than his guardian.

A thick cedar tree near the station cracked and, as he watched, it careened and fell towards the station. He jumped back as it smashed into the side of the structure. The glass exploded inward and the entire station shuddered. A second tree followed, crashing even harder into the side, destroying another window. It was as though this unseen beast was targeting its aggression and anger specifically at the station.

Of course, Tyler thought. *If it was a modified beast, it would be angry at all things human.* He needed to get out before the beast took the entire station down.

Tyler scrambled over to the hatch, pushing the items out of the way. He unlatched the lock as another tree pummeled the station. A loud crack sounded near Tyler, which he felt in his feet. It was the foundation that held the station to the tree base. He started to pull the hatch open when an even louder crack rang out and a portion of the roof collapsed. A thick tree that'd been dropped on top of the station blew through the structure, slamming Tyler to the floor.

The entire structure tilted at an angle steep enough that Tyler couldn't stand. Instead, when he tried to get back to his feet, he slipped and toppled sideways and crashed into the wall.

Another section of the roof was decimated as the creature ramped up its attack. This time the station became unmoored from its base. He had a moment of weightlessness before it slammed into the ground below. The impact sent him flying against the floor, which was now technically a wall, the structure having landed on its side. The creature roared and slammed into the downed shack, sending Tyler tumbling across the battered space.

An immense paw swiped at the shack, the claws easily splintering the wood and sending shrapnel flying all around.

Tyler scrambled back, looking for a way out. He found an opening and climbed onto one of the trees that had crashed through the roof. He scampered down the length of the tree and jumped to the ground once he was free from the building, running as fast as he could when he landed.

He didn't look back.

Weaving through the trees, he ran in different directions, struggling to create distance between him and his pursuer. The beast lumbered after him, snorting and grunting as it pushed through the forest. Tyler realized that while he was definitely creating issues for it, the creature wasn't being slowed much as it just crushed through the trees instead of going around them.

Tyler struggled to breathe, his body screaming at the

exertion. As he darted to the right a bolt of pain flashed through his head. His vision went blurry, then spun, before the dizziness hit him and a ringing sounded in his ears.

He fell to his knees, desperately trying to keep going. He was crawling, pulling himself along as his body revolted against the exertion. Stringy saliva was dripping from his open mouth. *Was he having a seizure? An aneurysm?*

Straining to look ahead, his vision cleared just enough to see a thinning of the trees.

It couldn't be? Could it?

From below the excruciating racket in his ears, he heard the beast approach and stop near his feet. Hot breath blew onto the back of his head and neck. Tyler waited to feel the inevitable puncture of the creature's teeth followed by being heaved into the air and shaken like a doll.

A few more feet. Was that Neil's voice urging him to not stop?

He grabbed onto roots and bushes, whatever his hands could find, and used them to pull, to force himself to keep going. Squinting he saw his only chance of survival.

Summoning all his strength and energy, using the hope of seeing his grandfather once more, he stood and ran.

It caught the beast off guard. Tyler made it a solid twenty feet before it ran.

He'd need to time this perfectly.

At the edge of the trees he slowed ever so slightly so that when the beast caught up to him, Tyler jumped to his left. The momentum of the beast carried it past where he'd jumped. It was able to stop quickly, but its size still placed it in the middle of the clearing.

To Tyler's disappointment nothing happened.

Instead he was getting his first good look at the demon bruin that was staring at him. He'd never seen anything this big before in nature. It would've easily crushed that lizard from the wall. An elephant would tremble before it.

Kneeling, Tyler began to say a final goodbye to the world. He'd gone so far, but ultimately he'd failed at finding his dad and failed at making it back to safety to reunite with his grandpa.

The beast's mouth opened and closed, a movement that made it appear to be smiling behind the short tusks and fangs that seemed to be everywhere. It took a step towards him when the spikes exploded from the ground. The sharp metal protrusions ripped through the innards of the creature, tearing it into a mass of viscera and fur. The death was so sudden and violent that it left Tyler stunned if not elated. He was so close to the edge of the clearing that he was splattered with blood, guts and fur.

He remained there, on his knees, for some time. Everything hurt. He wanted to stand, to start walking again, but even opening and closing his hands sent shockwaves up and down his arms. Wiggling his toes was akin to being electrocuted. He hadn't expected this to work. It'd been a risk he'd taken and here he sat, alive.

His head still throbbed, his heart still pounded, and his ears were still ringing. But he was alive.

Enough, he thought. Less pity. Time to get moving. He struggled to his feet, finding he was wobblier than he wanted.

Head injury. He had to remind himself that he wasn't just going to get over the head injury.

Tyler balanced himself against a tree, waiting until the forest was steady and he didn't feel like puking.

Returning to the destroyed station wasn't an option. It wasn't worth the risk to retrieve any water or food. The soldiers would most likely return, if they weren't there already. He thought about that sudden halt in the gun fire and the announcement of something incoming. The beast must have been tracked for them to be alerted. Which meant now, they would know where the beast had last been. It would also indicate, most likely, that the creature was dead.

The only option was to keep walking towards the perimeter. His destination kept moving further and further away.

47

———

Tyler continued to force himself to walk until the sun was directly above him.

The forest had grown silent, which made him uneasy. He didn't feel safe but knew he needed to take a break.

He hadn't heard any human sounds – no engines, shouts or gun fire – for some time. Now, Tyler didn't hear any animal sounds either.

Taking a seat by a downed tree, he stretched his legs out and shifted his back around so that the splintered ends didn't dig in. How he longed for an ice cold drink. Hell, even a warm drink would do.

Instead, he wiped the sweat off his forehead and licked what remained on his hand. The salty bits would dehydrate him even faster, but he needed something to moisten his mouth. The stubble of facial hair scratched his arm and he cringed. They were bright red. A sunburn covered much of his exposed skin, and having ditched the jacket a few miles back, he had nothing to shield the direct rays. Initially it had felt great to lose the weight of that jacket, and he was cooler the second he shrugged it off and tossed it on the ground, but now he wished he'd sucked it up and kept it on.

He had to admit, though, that it felt good to just sit.

A light breeze blew across him. Had he ever experienced anything so glorious? So refreshing? If he didn't know any better, Tyler would've believed he'd returned to that dream sitting on the beach with his parents.

It was time to go home.

As much as he'd be happy to sit here forever, the flicker of his parents smiling while he thought back to his dream was what got him standing and moving. The edge of the valley was getting closer. God, how he wanted to never set foot in this place ever again. He was confident that he'd make it to the base of that last hill by nightfall and, if he found the strength, Tyler might even make the effort to ascend to the top.

That would mean, in the morning, he'd only have the few miles to cross until he returned to the perimeter and another hour or so after that until he made it back to the SUV in the parking area. The perimeter itself gave him shivers. He knew Mr. Adams would be sending soldiers there to look for him, but he hoped maybe Carson had left a message for someone to look for him if he didn't return for his shift. Maybe some cops would be there, and even the media, to make sure Tyler safely crossed over, running into his grandpa's outstretched arms.

The SUV.

Tyler would break into a jog when he spotted it, he just knew. It would be like seeing a lover that you'd been away from for months. That moment of pure joy would overtake his aches and pains and he'd rush to that vehicle and hug it like it was a person.

He was walking faster now, returning to his usual, prehead-injury speed. He didn't know how long he could maintain this pace, but it meant he was covering more ground, getting closer and closer.

The path he was following wound through a denser section of cedars when the distinct sound of flowing water reached him.

A creek?

Buoyed by what might be ahead, he continued around the next corner and was rewarded with a sight that almost brought him to his knees. A bubbling creek crisscrossed in front of him. He could have cried, the sight was so beautiful. He rushed forward without a care in the world, stepping into the flowing fluid, and drank heartily from filled hands. He cupped them and brought the water to his mouth over and over, even as the water became so cold he could no longer feel his hands or feet. When he absolutely couldn't take any more, he hobbled on frozen feet to the other side, wiping the sloshed water that hadn't made it into his mouth from his face. He wished he had a canteen to fill. That simple thought felt like a gut punch to his stomach. Memories of Carson and that poor raccoon jumping back into his head.

As much as he wanted to sit at the water's edge and remain content, he needed to push those thoughts away and continue towards the perimeter. The water had done wonders on his aches and pains and even his resolve. His hunger was momentarily dampened. He knew he'd eat soon enough.

He was less than an hour from the valley wall. Nightfall wasn't too far behind that.

48

TYLER ARRIVED AT THE BASE OF THE VALLEY WALL WHEN TWO sounds got his attention.

The first was the muffled speech of people conversing. He wasn't sure exactly *where* they were, but he presumed it was soldiers patrolling somewhere ahead.

The second was more alarming than armed soldiers. It was the distinct noise of an animal huffing and pawing at the ground. It was very close. So close, in fact, that Tyler was certain if he looked over, he'd see it standing half-hidden in the trees beside him.

Ignoring the predator looming near, he started up the incline, working his way towards the top of the valley. When he'd entered this area, he'd had the foresight to follow an easy way down.

Now he didn't have that luxury.

Tyler did find the terrain was easy enough to climb and would have been significantly easier if he wasn't starving, dehydrated, and exhausted. Not to mention bruised, beaten, and still experiencing dizziness from his head injury.

From behind, the mystery creature kept pace, making

enough noise to remind him they were still there. Tyler looked back a few times, not surprised to see that it was keeping itself out of eye sight.

He arrived at the top of the valley wall, finding the muffled voices had grown louder. Tyler knew they were stationed at the perimeters edge. Waiting for him to arrive. What should've been an amazing moment considering everything he'd been through was more of the same. He needed to remain cautious.

Night had descended on the valley. Tyler longed to take one last look over the place. Even though he knew the exact location, he wouldn't be able to see the complex. It was too well hidden, camouflaged perfectly. But he'd never return and he wanted one last look, that last moment of connection between him and his parents. A final goodbye.

Instead, the snort of the beast got his legs moving. He didn't think he'd be able to navigate his way across the perimeter and down to the SUV in the dark, so he would need to find a hiding spot until the sun returned.

Tyler jogged ahead, wanting to try and ditch his follower. He entered a thick patch of bushes, cut to his right and pulled himself up into the branches of the nearest tree. The dark shape of the creature rushed by below, which let Tyler finally breathe out.

It was here he decided to sit and wait out the night. Tyler didn't think he'd actually sleep, fearful of falling from the tree. He also expected the beast to circle back around, trying to find just where he'd slipped away from it.

When morning came, it would be time to get to that SUV.

He wanted to go home.

49

Did he dream?

Tyler wasn't sure. He remembered *things* the next morning, events, but he wasn't sure whether real or dreamed.

The tree had moved, as though pushed. He'd had to grab on to stop from toppling off. An animal had roared and grunted in the dark. It had been close, but Tyler didn't know just where it was.

He also remembered thinking of his parents, hand in hand. He was on his dad's back as they hiked through the woods. They all laughed and his heart beat to a song he wasn't all that familiar with – completion.

But, of course, that was an illusion, a mirage his brain envisioned for him so that when Tyler woke to the birds singing and the sun shining it wasn't such a heartbreak to be alone, to be in pain and to struggle to move.

He climbed down from the tree. When he jumped from the bottom branch and landed, his knees failed and he fell to the ground in a heap, the pain beyond what he had anticipated.

Standing, he searched for any sign of his mystery

follower from the previous night, but he was alone. He stretched, the miles not willing to release from his muscles, but they loosened enough to know he'd be able to make it.

Tyler started walking towards where he'd crossed the perimeter all those days ago. He'd need to see if it was still being patrolled or guarded by soldiers, but at the moment he couldn't hear any voices to suggest it was.

He was surprised at how close he'd been to the edge of the perimeter. Looking, he easily located cameras and signage, as well as two men stationed at the exact place where he'd entered. They were standing with their arms resting on their assault rifles. Neither was speaking, instead looking around, keeping their eyes open for any movement, any sign of Tyler.

Crouching, his leg muscles fought his desire to lower himself. He couldn't stay in that position, so he put down a knee, resting his upper body on the other one.

God, he was tired.

He was also so very close to the SUV. His grandpa waited.

Looking at his options, he saw that there was a group of bushes close by that grew all the way to the trees, ending by the soldiers. He could crawl along the ground until there, then when they weren't watching, run to the other side of the path and hide in the deep grass, reversing most of what he did when he breached the line the first time.

Knowing that this was the best option and, truthfully, the only option, Tyler started to crawl. His back muscles were not happy being the prime movers now. The tight skin from his burn pulled with each movement, the collar of his shirt reminding him repeatedly. He had made it half the distance when the two soldiers both raised their rifles and took a shooting stance. He immediately ducked and closed his eyes, waiting for the sharp pain of a bullet and the end of his life. When that didn't happen, he stole a glance.

They weren't aiming at Tyler. Instead they were both pointed straight ahead, facing the direction of the valley beyond. A violent roar cascaded through the area, followed by the sound of something large crashing nearby.

The two soldiers opened fire, their rifles snapping with each burst of pressure on the trigger. Tyler didn't care what they were firing at. Instead he used it to his advantage and as cover to get up and run. He stayed close to the bushes and kept glancing at the two soldiers, hoping they wouldn't see him.

The two took another step forward, continuing to fire at the approaching creature. Its roars had increased in volume, but there was now a different tone in them, a pained sound that affected Tyler far more than it should have.

He didn't stop.

Tyler scampered across the perimeter and continued down the path. He didn't think for a second that the soldiers wouldn't follow him or that other soldiers, alerted to him breaching the perimeter and attempting to escape, wouldn't be in hot pursuit. Tyler just wanted to get to the SUV, to get in and drive away, leaving the horror and the heartache behind him.

Grandpa.

He kept a picture of the smiling man in his head as he pushed his body to the absolutely limit. This was it. Tyler's last stand. He would arrive at the SUV, get in and that would be it. He'd have no more to give, but at that point the engine would take over.

He knew he'd have a hospital stay in his future. Treatment for dehydration, his burns, his injuries. He'd have months and years ahead with therapists and counsellors, all giving him tools to try and work through his PTSD as well as the anxiety he would have for the rest of his life.

But none of that was *now*.

Everything came back. The layout of the trail system, the way it looped and came around to the parking lot. The odd roots and rocks that created natural steps.

The sounds of gunfire had ended. Tyler was shocked that he didn't hear heavy footsteps behind him as the soldiers gained.

Instead, it was just him, his feet pounding the ground, his breaths in and out creating the impression that a freight train was making its way through the mountain terrain.

Then, there, ahead, the parking area.

Tyler started crying as he stumbled and fell. He didn't want to get back up but he was so close to the end. He staggered from the trees and entered the parking area. His vehicle was the lone occupant of the space. It sat right where he'd left it, and even from fifty feet he could see it was covered with a layer of dust. He was shocked it was still there, half expecting Mr. Adams to have had it towed.

Much like Tyler had imagined, he broke into a dead sprint, ready to hug and kiss the vehicle.

He was here! Here! He'd arrived. Somehow, he had survived. When he got to the SUV, he couldn't actually believe it was real. He ran his hands over the hood and the door.

Then he grabbed the handle and pulled.

It was locked.

He reached for his backpack to grab the keys and his entire world came crashing down.

The backpack.

Something had been nagging him about the pack since escaping the complex, something important and here it was.

How could this be? Here he stood beside the SUV, ready to escape, ready to drive away and never come back, but it couldn't happen. The pack that he needed was gone.

Tyler's head spun, his knees wobbled, and he would've passed out then and there if it wasn't for the voice that spoke from behind him.

"Tyler? Son?"

He turned, knowing exactly what he'd find but wishing against everything that it wasn't going to be real. The creature that used to be his father stood a dozen feet away.

"My boy," the creature said, stepping towards him with outstretched appendages. "It's time you come join us."

A noise from his left let him know a moment before a soldier brought the end of their rifle down against his face.

Tyler crumpled to the ground.

50

———

The howling of wind accompanied by the sound of the rain brought him back.

Tyler came to in a cave, naked.

He rolled over and sat, his head throbbing from yet another blow.

He looked around, finding the surroundings all too familiar. He knew the names would be carved into the wall at the back without even checking.

Getting as close to a standing position as he could, he walked to the bars made of branches at the front. He looked from his cell at the forest beyond.

He wanted to scream, to cry, to break these bars open and pitch himself off the side of the mountain, but he knew that wouldn't happen.

Instead, a soldier would come. Tyler would be bound and transported to the complex where a doctor and their crew would decide on what to turn him into. At least then he'd rejoin his parents.

I should be happy, he thought. *We'll be reunited at least.*

But deep down, that wasn't true.

So, Tyler returned to the back of the cave and began to sob.

His life, as he knew it, was over.

Sadly, he'd never be ready for what was to come.

As the tears came harder, far off in the distance, an all too familiar bellow sounded.

This time, his guardian wouldn't be able to save him.

EPILOGUE

GOLDEN STAR JUNE 17TH, 2007

RCMP still have no leads.

What started out as an abandoned vehicle call has baffled Golden RCMP. After attempting to contact the owner of the abandoned SUV in the parking area near the trails leading towards Ogre Peak, RCMP still have no idea as to the location of Tyler Barton nor their own missing member, Officer Rich Carson. "It's as though they both just disappeared," said acting media liaison, Officer Janson.

Officer Janson asked that any hikers entering the area keep an eye out for any signs of the two, but that currently, Golden RCMP are considering the case closed without any leads.

END.

AFTERWORD

In April of 2020, I, like many people in the world, was temporarily laid off from my work place as the beginning of the Covid-19 Pandemic restrictions came into place. At the time, here in Edmonton, where I worked was deemed non-essential and for eight weeks I was sent home, before slowly returning to modified hours and eventually full time. I work in the medical field, so I was happy to return to work and be able to see my patients again and help them remain active and pain free.

While I was stressed over not working, at the same time it offered me a rare opportunity to spend more time with my wife, son and our dog. I mentioned almost immediately to my wife that I'd need to figure out a way to keep working on my current works in progress, and she suggested that each day, I still take that hour I normally write at work and do that at home. I was also able to find other open spaces where I wrote and it was during those eight weeks I cranked out the first draft of this book. Draft one sat at a little over 42K words.

As I usually do, I let the novel sit for a month before I

opened the file again and worked on draft two. Sadly, this coincided with my father-in-law unexpectedly passing away in June. An incredibly emotional time, which we're still trying to navigate, I knew I could utilize some of those emotions I was working through, and my wife was sharing, to add into Tyler's journey here.

While many authors have different metaphors or meanings in their work, they usually don't discuss them, allowing the reader to have their own journey.

Indulge me if you will, as I take a brief moment to discuss one of those metaphors. Having finished writing this – I'm confident that I have three metaphors at play here, but the one I'll discuss is my search for meaning.

When the pandemic hit, I felt lost. Alone. Depressed. Much like many other people out there. We are a single income family. This was something we decided when we discovered we were going to be parents. For us, it worked better that I kept working and my wife stayed home and raised him. When the pandemic hit, we had a lot of what 'ifs.' This book was cathartic for me, in that I metaphorically explored this concept. It gave me some much needed purpose and mental distraction and for that, I'm so thankful for this novel.

The cover art on this release is done by the fantastic François Vaillancourt. I've long been a fan of his creations and it was one day where this came across one of his posts and I knew this had been specifically made for this book. It was fate (or Ka, for you constant readers). François was so easy to work with and I can't thank him enough or recommend him enough.

Huge thanks to Mason McDonald, who'd actually made me some promotional graphics as well as an original cover. I showed this to Mason and he said "use it." We both knew it matched this story so well. Mason is a great writer, phenomenal cover artist and someone I'm thankful to call my friend.

When the internet slowly began to become a thing for me, back in the early 00's, I used to visit cryptozoology.com all the time. I don't even know if that's still a site or not, but when I first saw the footage of the Mammoth (or Mastodon!) shared there or on a similar site, I was blown away. I believe it's been debunked or proven to be a hoax/fake, but to this day, when I watch that clip I get tingly all over. I want something like that to be real so badly, that I always get excited. The wilderness is a vast and amazing place, so I hold the hope that it's a possibility. The clip Tyler mentions and I'm referencing can be found here;

https://www.youtube.com/watch?v=8UtHUoiGRjQ (Mammoth crosses river)

This book is also a massive love letter to my home province, British Columbia. The world is vast and mighty, but B.C. is beauty like nowhere else. Throughout, I also gave some nods to friends from when we lived in the Lower Mainland. I mention Tyler and Neil going to Cultus Lake where Neil has a friend with a shop. My buddy Jody has a tattoo shop in Cultus. Love him like a brother. Tyler mentions to Carson about a friend of his dad's flying a plane in Squamish. That would be my friend David, who not only is a pilot, but was also my main bobsled pilot when I was a slider. Mr. Adams was loosely a reference to my good, good friend, Steve. And lastly, Harry who I mention took photos in Golden, is a friend of mine who was actually from Golden and moved to the coast.

As for the location – the places are real, but I highly doubt there is a hidden government complex there. Well, I guess we never truly know. Ogre Peak is only about 50 km from the town of Golden, BC, but it takes about three hours to get there. I took liberties with the travel time in the story. The co-ordinates of Ogre Peak are 51.551434 N - 116.730556 W for those curious and the peak is 9,278 feet high. Twin Lakes lies at the base of Ogre Peak in a South East direction. The co-ordinates for the larger of the two lakes is 51.542109 N - 116.715379 W, for those who would be curious to visit. Twin Lakes is a known back packing place and the photos I've seen of the area online are gorgeous.

In a way, this was my attempt at re-telling or creating my own 'The Island of Doctor Moreau.' Whether I was successful is left up to you, reader.

I want to say thanks to everyone who has always supported me and my work; the writing, the reviewing and the random stuff I get up to. Nora, Char, Jen, Chris, Shane, Toni, Laurie, Beard, Brad, Randall and so, so many more!

Thanks to Gavin. You're a good friend, mate.

Thanks as always to David Sodergren. Cheers to 'The Navajo Nightmare.' I never thought I'd get an Amazon Banner, but to get one and to share that success with you - I'll never forget that.

Cheers to Robert and Sarah at 7th Terrace for your kindness.

To Stacey Kondla, thank you for your notes and your time, it meant the world!

Thanks to so many amazing writers who've become friends. I'm probably missing a few, but - J.H. Moncrieff, Duncan Ralston, D.W. Gillespie, Justin M. Woodward, RJ Roles, Ross Jeffery, J.R. McConvery, Alan Baxter, Bo Chappell, A.A. Median, John Bender, B.P Gregory, Kev Harrison, Sean O'Connor, Adam Nevill, Ronald Malfi, Alyson Faye, Tim Lebbon, Lee Murray, Brian Fatah Steele, Andrew Cull, Sonora Taylor, and Laurel Hightower for your kindness and support.

To Andrew Pyper. I'm still blown away that my favorite author knows my name and that he calls me a friend. I attended an online workshop of his which really helped to iron out some issues I was having with this book, but also two other novels. His input was amazing. I was hesitant on reaching out to see if he'd offer a blurb if he enjoyed this, but when I mentioned it to my wife, she said I absolutely needed to ask. I was raving about this book and she knew how much this book meant to me and that I'd kick myself if I didn't. To think that he read this and enjoyed it AND offered a blurb! Blown away. Thank you, and I'll continue to post pictures of your work forever haha!

To Shaun Hamill, Eddie Generous, Joseph Sale, Jennifer Sullivan (TOC BUDDIES!) and David Sodergren, thank you for your kind words.

Thank you to Amanda and Auryn. You two are the best things in my life and I love you both to the moon and back.

Lastly, thank you, OJ. God, how I miss you. You were the best dog. I wrote the first version of this afterword on May 5, 2021, which was the 9th anniversary of when I picked you up and about six weeks since I saw you last. Every single day, until your final day was a gift and you made our lives so much better. You were with us for a long time, but not long enough. I'm so happy that you started to love Auryn like you did in the last year you were with us, because God knows how much Auryn loved you. We still talk about you, I hope you know that. We'll always talk about you.

I went through this draft in the weeks after you passed away, and you infused so much of how I approached Tyler and Neil's journey. I'll stop there. It's always awkward when you can tell someone's crying while they type something.

OJ – I love you, buddy. You were the best chrome dome ever.

I'll leave it there.

I'd love it if you'd consider leaving a rating or even a few words on Amazon, Goodreads or Bookbub. Good or bad. Always appreciated.

Until we meet again,

Steve

Edmonton, AB

December 6th, 2021

WRITING PLAYLIST

I typically listen to very dark, heavy music while writing, but I found for this novel, I needed to take a different route. I had an all-Canadian playlist as well as an electronic playlist.

Canadian Playlist;

Arcade Fire – Everything Now, The Suburbs, Wake Up, Keep the Car Running

The Trews – Time's Speeding Up, Sing Your Heart Out, Rise in the Wake, Not Ready to Go, Tired of Waiting

Wintersleep – Weighty Ghost

The Strumbellas – Spirits, We Don't Know

Sam Roberts – Brother Down

Big Sugar – If I Had My Way

The Tragically Hip – Ahead by a Century, Lake Fever

The Tea Party - Stargazer

Electronic Playlist;

Above and Beyond – See the End, Tight Rope, Second Chance, Peace of Mind

3LUA – Tokyo

Missio – Bottom of the Deep Blue See

Gryffin – All You Need to Know

Gunship – When You Grow Up, Your Heart Dies, Dark All Day

MGMT – Kids, Time to Pretend

Anabel Englund – So Hot, Waiting For You

ABOUT THE AUTHOR

Steve Stred writes dark, bleak fiction.

Steve is the author of a number novels, novellas and collections.

He is proud to work with the Ladies of Horror Fiction to facilitate the Annual LOHF Writers Grant.

Steve has appeared alongside Horror's heaviest hitters in some fantastic anthologies.

He is an active member of the HWA.

He is based in Edmonton, AB, Canada and lives with his wife and son.

Website: stevestredauthor.wordpress.com

ALSO BY STEVE STRED

Novels

- Invisible
- The Stranger
- Piece of Me (Sermons of Sorrow Book 1)
- The Navajo Nightmare (co-written with David Sodergren)
- Incarnate

Novellas

- Jane: the 816 Chronicles
- Wagon Buddy
- YURI
- The Girl Who Hid In the Trees
- Ritual (Father of Lies Book 1)
- COMMUNION (Father of Lies Book 2)
- Sacrament (Father of Lies Book 3)
- The Window In the Ground
- The One That Knows No Fear
- Scott: A Wagon Buddy Tale
- Wound Upon Wound
- The Future In the Sky (The Empyrean Saga Book 1)
- The Boy Whose Room Was Outside

Collections

- Frostbitten: 12 Hymns of Misery
- Left Hand Path: 13 more tales of black magick
- Dim the Sun
- The Night Crawls In

- Of Witches...
- Father of Lies: The Complete Series Omnibus

www.ingramcontent.com/pod-product-compliance
Lightning Source LLC
Chambersburg PA
CBHW070415310726
48977CB00003B/699